"Are you going to tell me I have to get out of town?"

Fowler's eyebrow lifted. "How'd you know that?"

Harlan laughed. "I knew it when I whipped Anders this afternoon. I looked at him laying there and I knew by tonight he'd be drunk, telling people to tell me I have twenty-four hours to get out of town. I never built a railroad yet that some hothead didn't give me twenty-four hours. That's my lucky number.

"Tell you something else," he went on. "Right now Anders is kneeling by his bed, praying I'll get out of town and he won't be stuck with his brag."

"I don't know," Fowler said. "He's a tough customer. And there are others . . ."

"Go to bed," Harlan said. "I'm going to spend tomorrow night between clean sheets, not in rock salt. I don't know about Anders. That's up to him . . ."

FRANK BONHAM

RAWHIDE GUNS

BERKLEY BOOKS, NEW YORK

RAWHIDE GUNS

A Berkley Book / published by arrangement with
the author

PRINTING HISTORY
Berkley edition / September 1978
Second printing / April 1981

ISBN: 0-425-04815-2

A BERKLEY BOOK® TM 757,375

CHAPTER 1

HARLAN SAT on the platform of the private car called *Rio Arriba*. His boots rested on the brass guard rail as he gazed down the converging strips of rust of the branchline. In shirt sleeves, a tall, well-built man of twenty-eight with gray eyes and dark hair, Harlan rocked slightly on the rear legs of the chair. He had waited an hour and a half for a man who was supposed to be here when he arrived, and impatience had begun to tighten in him like a muscular cramp.

Jim Harlan had noticed that money made some men careless about promises. Senator Tom Sorrell had more money than most men, so perhaps he was more careless. A man Harlan had thought a great deal of used to tell him, "Never let a man keep you waiting, Jim. It makes you his flunky." Harlan settled his Stetson on the side of his head and thought, Maybe we'll have to get straightened out on who's going to be whose flunky, Senator.

A moody-eyed man carrying a long-snouted oil can stopped beside the platform. "Burning up a lot of coal, Mr. Harlan."

"We'll get started," Harlan promised. "I keep thinking that wire will come."

He continued waiting. He was going to build a railroad in the Magdalena Basin, ten miles south of this junction town, La Cinta, New Mexico Territory. Senator Sorrell had secured the charter for him several months ago, when he was finishing a term in the Territorial senate. Yesterday, just before he left Santa Fe, Jim Harlan had received a wire from Sorrell, requesting a meeting at La Cinta. Sorrell was not supposed to have had anything to do with Harlan's securing a charter; ostensibly they were not even ac-

1

quainted. Jim Harlan wondered how Sorrell thought their meeting could be made to appear accidental, now.

Sooty tatters of coal smoke whipped past the platform. Nearby, some milch goats grazed. Along the tracks were a dozen shacks built of railroad ties rooted end-up and chinked with mud. Tinted with the green of early spring, the high mesa ran south, to crumble in a relief map of deep bays and lofty peninsulas, like catwalks into the Magdalena Basin. Mesas like hats lay on the horizon. It was a land where a wind could work up enthusiasm, where a wheeling buzzard stood out like a fly on a plastered wall.

Suddenly Harlan took his boots off the railing and leaned forward. A small herd of cattle had begun to scramble up out of an arroyo near the village. Harlan immediately recognized the rider with them as Senator Sorrell. Sorrell was a very large man with square shoulders and an outdoor look. He wore a military mustache and had the face of an Army officer, keen, abrupt, and intelligent. His eyes touched Jim and then flicked on to the loading pens, as though he had not seen him, as though he did not remember the time in Santa Fe, a few months ago, when he had set up the plan for Jim Harlan to build this Magdalena Basin railroad.

Jim sat back. I can wait as long as you, mister, he decided. But come with your hat in your hands.

He cleaned his nails with a golden pen-knife. They were frosty with cleaning. All at once he looked up. This is nonsense, he thought. Maybe he was held up. But blast it, there was no sense in starting at the last minute! Sorrell had arranged the meeting, not he. On the other hand, Jim conceded grudgingly, he might have a perfectly good excuse.

He closed the knife and frowned as he tossed it on his hand. What was it in Tom Sorrell which irritated him? In Santa Fe, Sorrell had been an amiable companion. But Jim never really got close to him. When Sorrell walked into a room, it was like a judge entering a courtroom. You felt you should rise. He laughed at your joke and told his own, but somehow you might say he kept his counter stool between you and him. And yet Jim could not be sure whether this was true or whether it was merely a jealous kink in his own mind. There had been a lot of hunger and home-made boots in Jim Harlan's boyhood. Although it had been some time, now, since Jim had asked the price of anything he wanted to buy, he still did not feel quite easy with men of wealth.

Tom Sorrell, having told the stationmaster how he wanted the gates handled, wheeled as if to return to his herd. But as he passed the long railroad car, he appeared to notice it for the first time. He drew rein. Jim watched him. At last Sorrell's gaze found him.

"Pretty fancy, mister." He smiled. "Always travel this way?"

"It's the only way," Jim said. "The railroad car isn't made that's big enough for more than two people. How's the ballast on the Magdelena Grade, Senator?"

Sorrell shook his head warningly. "Watch out, Jim. You aren't supposed to know me, remember."

Jim raised an eyebrow. "Shoot, Senator, everybody knows you. Isn't that your picture on the Old Congress whiskey bottle?"

Sorrell spoke in dry reprimand. "Don't wear yourself out being funny, Jim. We've got a lot to talk about, and mighty little time."

"We'd have more time," Jim said, "if you'd kept our appointment."

A muscle flickered in Sorrell's jaw. "Will you keep your voice down? If anyone gets the idea there's anything between us, it'll go straight to Cameron Travis. And I can tell you right now it'll be easier to work with him than against him."

Smiling, Jim stood up. "Can't you handle Travis? I hear he's seventy years old."

"I can handle him. I can break rocks with my fist, too, but I know easier ways."

"Come on in and tell me some of them," Jim invited.

When Sorrell entered the sitting room of the private car, Jim was pouring drinks at a sideboard. The room was elegant with mahogany and moss-green drapes. Jim handed Sorrell his drink and the rancher grinned and punched him lightly on the chin. "Get off that high horse, Jim. We're amigos, aren't we?" Then he sniffed the whiskey and said, "Say, this is my label! You must have known I was coming."

"I was beginning to wonder," Jim said.

"I'm sorry. I should have left last night and camped out."

Undisturbed, Sorrell relaxed in a horsehair armchair. He cocked one leg across his knee, hung his Stetson on the toe of his boot and sighed loudly. It was hard to dislike Tom Sorrell, Jim decided. Self-assured, sunburned and hearty, he was good company. Glancing about the room, Sorrell seemed to take hold of the situation as he might grasp a rope. It made Jim uneasy. Sorrell was one of those men who would move in on you and take over, and Jim wanted to run this show himself.

The rancher glanced at him. ''Mrs. Sorrell sends her good wishes, by the way.''

Jim's gaze wavered, then steadied, and he bowed his head. ''Thanks. How is Mrs. Sorrell?''

''Lovena is fine. She said to tell you to hurry your work so we can bring our friendship into the open and have you to dinner.''

''If I needed an excuse to hurry, that would be it. I'll look forward to it.''

''I'll tell her you said that,'' Sorrell said, and added, ''She loves a compliment.''

Jim looked into the rancher's eyes. What did that mean? Lovena Sorrell had been with her husband in Santa Fe when Sorrell was pushing for Jim's railroad charter. Sorrell rarely took her on his business trips, she said. She had a dainty, dark-eyed beauty, and was very young, scarcely twenty, the daughter of an officer of the Great Southern Railroad. Twice Sorrell had brought Jim up to their hotel suite on business, and each time Sorrell had been late. Once Jim and Lovena had spent an hour alone together. You had to apply the crinoline word, demure, to Sorrell's young wife. But she was more than that. She was intelligent and curious. She couldn't stand being alone and she seemed to encourage Jim to pay her compliments, but in the most proper way possible. No intimate word had ever passed between them, yet Jim was convinced that she wanted him to touch her, to try to kiss her, so she could turn him down. In this way she could prove her virtue but achieve a conquest. Jim wondered how foolish Tom Sorrell really was where his wife was concerned. She needed company, and if Sorrell did not supply it, sooner or later some other man would.

Sorrell, glancing about the room, asked curiously:

''What do you expect to have out of this little railroad you're going to build, Jim?''

''Money,'' Jim said.

"You don't mean that." Sorrell chided good-naturedly. "You really want to be like Jim Hull or somebody, don't you? Prestige, and empire, and all?"

Now Jim remembered what it was he disliked about the rancher. He did not like to be patronized.

"No," Jim said. "No empires or prestige for me. I'm out for the quick dollar—just like a rancher going to the senate. Or did you want to be like Henry Clay?"

Sorrell sipped the whiskey. "Jim," he said soberly, "we aren't setting out to be very good friends, are we?"

"Do we have to be good friends to work together? I had a friend who helped organize an army of Mexican rebels. He and the general hated each other, but they worked together fine."

"Your friend got shot." Sorrell smiled.

"I didn't get shot," Jim said. "I don't think I'm going to get shot, either. I figure you must want me to build this railroad or you wouldn't have gotten me a charter."

"Using your head, Jim," Sorrell approved.

"Another thing my head's working on," Jim mentioned, "is why you wired me to meet you here."

"To warn you not to tip your hand to Cam Travis that I set things up for you," Sorrell replied. "You've got to get right-of-way through his land, and if he won't give it to you, no other rancher in the basin will let you cross his land either."

"You told me that before."

"I wasn't sure I emphasized it. Cam Travis and I—well, the way things are between us, he drinks at the Gold Exchange and I patronize the Cloverleaf. We can't even agree on saloons. And of course he likes Black Angus cattle and I run to whitefaces. When it comes to hay land he's an irrigation man and I'm dry land. Irrigation brings squatters. They come up out of the muck, like mosquitoes. Let Travis know I got you your charter, and he'll set every rancher in the valley against you."

Jim shrugged. "I'm not afraid of Travis. Are you?"

Sorrell's leather-brown eyes watched him with cool amusement. "I'm not afraid of any man I can predict—and I can predict Cam Travis like the weather."

"Predict me," Jim suggested.

"I already have. But I keep my predictions secret. Why encourage people to get hurt trying to prove I'm wrong? The whole point is, if Cam gets the idea there's anything irregular about this railroad of yours, he'll tie you head-down on a blind horse and give it the quirt."

They had never discussed the peculiar circumstance that a man as young as Jim Harlan, with no tangible assets, should be promoting and building a railroad. They had ignored it as one made one's self deaf to a stranger's stammer. Harlan had needed a charter. He had been sent to Sorrell as the man who could get it for him.

Jim said innocently, "What's irregular about my railroad?"

"Nothing, I hope," Sorrell said blandly. "I wouldn't have had anything to do with it if there were." He tapped the rowel of his spur and it rang like money. "Scared, Jim?" he asked.

"I don't think so. A shade excited. This is a pretty big thing, for a little fellow like me."

"I'll bet you never built anything bigger than a pair of jacks in your life!" Sorrell laughed.

"There isn't anything bigger," Jim assured him. "All you ever need is jacks to open—and the guts to back them."

"Is that what happened down there in Mexico?" Sorrell asked. "Did you open on jacks and back them too long?"

Jim hesitated. "They changed administrations, and we were in midstream," he confessed. "Sullivan and I picked the wrong side to build a railroad for. He got the firing squad because he'd done some recruiting, and I got ten years. But they took their eyes off me for a minute."

. . . And afterward, never having felt so alone, missing deeply the man who had taught him how to be fast on his feet, who had instructed him in the art of not being poor, and had been the best friend he would ever have, Jim had left Mexico. He was glad he had got into the railroad thing so quickly.

"Well, it's rough game, being a soldier of fortune," Sorrell said. *Rough,* his face said, *and no trade for a gentleman.* "I'll have to get back," he said. He settled his Stetson and sauntered to the door. "By the way," he said, "it might be a good idea for you to make regular reports to me. I'll kind of keep you straightened out on what you can do and what you can't do."

. . . It was now perfectly plain why he had summoned Jim to the La Cinta meeting: He wanted the wave of the saber which started the battle to be his gesture. He had some secret stake in this gamble of Jim's, and he meant to keep control of it.

"Thanks," Jim said, "but I wouldn't know how to make a report. I've always lone-wolfed it."

Sorrell's dark skin flushed. "Suit yourself," he said brusquely. But then he added, "I might be useful, you know. I'm pretty good at stalling bill collectors, in case any of those back debts catch up with you."

"I'm solvent," Jim said.

Again Sorrell smiled, but anger and impatience were in his eyes. He was showing himself to Jim more than he ever had. Sorrell could be fast and hard and dangerous. "I had an idea you were probably one jump ahead of the marshal," he said. "Most men in your trade are."

Jim returned his gaze. Then he turned his hand palmdown, made his fist and showed him the large ruby ring he wore. "I can raise a thousand on that any time I want," he said. "I could buy and sell most men in my trade—as you call it."

"Good, Jim!" Sorrell applauded. "Good for you." Then a faint frown made a tuck between his eyes. "Jim, I hope you won't misunderstand me. But people who are used to money—people of quality, like Cam Travis,—well, they don't talk about how much they own. I only mention it so you won't offend him right off," he explained.

Jim felt the cold drench of his shame and anger. He had been feinted into boastfulness and then given a lesson in manners. Sorrell was making it plain that he looked on Jim as a barbarian. Jim watched him ride away. People of quality! Quality, to Sorrell, was what you carried in your billfold. Honesty and loyalty had nothing to do with it.

He wished he were not beholden to Sorrell for his charter. Sorrell thought he owned him because of it. He was so sure of himself, of everything he owned; and the things he owned were often men. Jim realized now that it had been insubordination to refuse to be master-minded by him. He must feel pretty sure of his wife, too, to leave her alone as he did. A warm memory awoke in Jim. She wanted me to kiss her, he thought. She wouldn't have let me, but she wanted me to try.

For so short a time, he had become very fond of her. He used to wake at night and think of her. He had decided finally that the less he saw of Lovena, the better. Falling in love with married women was a folly suited to other men, not to Jim Harlan.

Now, how did I get on this, he wondered. He knew, though, and was ashamed to have thought of Mrs. Sorrell as a way of getting back at the senator. Jim walked into the platform and leaned over the side. He called to a trainman, ''never mind the telegram. Let's go.''

CHAPTER 2

THE TRAIN pushed its short string of mixed cars down the plain. Water had found a weakness in the mesa, and centuries of erosion had rabbetted out the Magdalena Basin, a thousand feet below the plain. The clawmarks of old floods remained. Fragile ribs of land, rising red from the floor of the basin and capped with green, left deep canyons between them as they projected into the basin. Down one of these canyons the old tracks of the Magdalena Short Line wandered like a lost dog. Silver and china jingled the length of Jim Harlan's car. Standing apprehensively on the platform, he waited for the train to stumble on a blind sag and flounder into the willows. But the old ballast was as solid as rock. Whoever had laid these tracks down must have meant to travel over them himself. Suddenly the train emerged on a bluff above a great armful of rolling, broken land. Jim was impressed. There was scarcely a place for your eye to stop rambling.

Deep in the south, mountains like sleeping cats curled about the basin, and somewhere across the mountains was Silver City, where his railroad would end. Down here it was another climate. Trees and grass were protected from the scouring winds of the high mesa. It was warm and still and the grass and leaves gleamed like ice in the sun. His eye followed lettuce-green clouds of poplars along the rivers.

Cameron Travis had said in a letter that he would meet Jim at Travis Siding, which was the end of the line. As the train chowed on, feeling its way, Jim began to look for the siding. The rails curled about a hillside, the wheels clicked under Jim's platform, and the

9

weeds scraping the bottom of the car smelled like molasses. All at
once there was a jolt. Jim had to clutch the guardrail to keep his
balance. Another impact jarred the car. He heard of a piece of china
crash somewhere. The train was already stopping.

They walked along the grade and tested with shovels. Jim saw a
dense growth of pine-grass, and right away he knew what had
happened.

"There's a seep in the hillside," he said. "The water collects
under the tracks. I'll walk ahead and scout it."

But a few yards farther along there was no bottom at all to the mud
and he flagged the train down. "We'll have to dig it out and get
some rocks under the ties," he said.

While the train crew started to work, he walked on, probing at the
grade with the handle of the shovel. The tracks followed the shoulder of the hill. In a short time the train was out of sight. The seep
dried up, but Jim kept walking because he was stale from riding.
Not far ahead, the rails made a tight right turn, came back a quarter
of a mile below, and cut left across a stream. He looked down on the
trestle, which was less than a quarter of a mile away, and then he
saw the man and woman standing on the tracks just short of the
trestle.

He watched them for a while before he understood that the man
was loosening a rail. He thought, I'll be damned.

With a bar, the man was prying the rail out of line. He wore chaps
and a striped jersey. Nearby stood a saddle pony and a horse and
buggy. The girl was watching with the back of one hand on her hip.
She made a motion with her free hand.

"I *will* be damned!" Jim said aloud. It was funny. But it would
not have been funny to pitch into that dry stream bed. What puzzled
him was that anyone should resent his coming enough to try to
wreck his train. He watched them for a few moments, then started
down the hillside toward the bridge.

The man and girl had their backs to Jim. He reached the lower set
of tracks. Quietly he approached, and soon he heard the man say, as
he straightened to massage his back, "By George, that ought to do
it!"

"A little more, I think, Chet," the girl said. She was slender and
had nice, womanly hips and blond hair with a wash of red in it.

There was something fetching about the way she stood with the back of her hand on her hip. She looked as though she were arranging furniture. She tilted her head as she gazed at the rail, trying to be sure about it. Jim moved up, walking on the ties so they would not hear him. The cowboy in the black-and-white jersey glanced at the girl.

"*More,* Miss Hester? Any more and they'll notice it sure."

"Of course, Chet. I want them to. We don't want a wreck, do we? We just want to—to let them know they aren't wanted."

The man laid the bar back over his shoulder. "Don't we? You're the boss, but I'd like a wreck fine."

"Chet, you're terrible." The girl laughed.

"You called it that time, Miss Hester," Jim said. "He is terrible, for a fact." They both jumped and looked around. He stood there with the skirts of his corduroy coat pushed back and his hands on his hips, tall and relaxed and grinning with ugly intensity.

"Oh!" the girl gasped. Her eyes were the darkest blue Jim could remember seeing. She put her fingertips to her cheek. Jim sauntered on.

"You'd like a wreck fine, would you?" he said to the cowboy. The man had not spoken nor stirred, but he had shaken off his surprise like a punch to the chin. He began to grin. He was not tall, but burly and muscular. He wore his hat over one ear and the way he held the pry-bar told Jim he did not intend to apologize.

"Sure, I like a little old wreck now and then," he said. "I mean, not as a steady diet, but for other people they're fine."

"Not when I'm one of the other people," Jim said. "Who are you?"

"You can call me Chet," the cowboy said. "That's if I can call you Jim."

Jim glanced at the girl, who was still pale and silent. "How'd you know I was Jim Harlan?" he asked the man.

"Knew you were coming, Jim, and I allowed you'd be wearing a corduroy coat and carryin' a slide rule in your pocket, to prove you were a railroad man instead of a stock promoter."

"*Are* you Mr. Harlan?" the girl asked suddenly.

"Yes, ma'am. I want to thank you for trying to give me an even chance to avoid a wreck. But I'd like it if you and your friend would start putting that tie back where it was.''

The girl bit her lip. "Chet, I think we'll have to."

Chet lowered the pry-bar. "Miss Hester," he protested, "we ain't takin' orders from this fella! He don't own these tracks."

"But neither do we. Please do as he asks. I wouldn't want any trouble with Uncle Cam." She turned to Jim. "Will you forget about this if we put the rail back?"

"Deal," said Jim. "You'd better hurry, though, because my train will be along in a few minutes."

He sat down to chew on a straw of tobosa grass. Uncle Cam, she'd said. So she was Travis' niece. Chet, staring in glittering hostility at Jim, lifted and dropped the bar, making chisel marks on a tie.

Hester took the pry-bar from him, and, with feminine distaste for tools, began to try to move the tie. Chet took the bar and pushed her aside. He braced his feet and put his shoulders to the job. The girl wiped her hands daintily on her skirts. Jim smiled at her and plucked another tobosa stem, which he offered her.

Hester shook her head. She was under strong pressure. "Mr. Harlan, don't you know why we were doing this?"

"To give me the idea I'm not wanted. I heard you. But I haven't added up why you don't want me."

Hester glanced across the basin with wistful shadows in her eyes. There was a spattering of small freckles on her nose. She looked like a sweet and sincere girl, and Jim felt sorry for her.

"Well," she said finally. "I'm Hester Travis. Cameron Travis is my uncle. This is Chet Anders. He's my uncle's foreman."

Anders' gaze came up. Then he wiped his mouth and went back to work. Distantly, a train hooted.

"Do you know who built this railroad you're traveling over?" Hester asked.

"I believe your uncle did. At least, ownership of it is in his name. I mean to buy it from him," he explained. "I don't see why all the excitement in that direction."

"That's not it. It's just—well, do legitimate railroad men often build railroads in places they've never been?"

Jim chewed on the straw. "Ma'am, it's like buying stock in a mine you've never seen. You can learn all you need to know from assayers' and geologists' reports. I've read everything on the Magdalena Basin. I'm convinced my road will be a money-maker, even though your uncle had the misfortune to go broke."

"Knowing my uncle failed in this short line of his, aren't you afraid you'll fail too?"

"I'm not going to fail, Miss Hester," Jim said reasonably. "I know exactly what I'm up against."

"Did you know you were up against Great Southern Railroad?"

"A little fish like me? No!"

"You are, though. Uncle Cam didn't know he was, either, until he began to have construction troubles. He tried to interest Great Southern in buying him out, but they wouldn't. Then he tried to get the Territory to help him, but Great Southern lobbied that down. Finally, when he gave up and decided to use the road just to ship out cattle and bring in supplies, they refused to take his freight on the main line."

Jim had not heard this, and Hester must have seen his surprise in his face. One of the things he could not tell her about his railroad was that Great Southern was backing him. Even he and Sorrell had not discussed this. Great Southern had told Jim, when they first contacted him, that someone in the basin had it in for them and would hold them up on right-of-way charges if they went in under their own name. So Jim was to build the railroad and re-sell to Great Southern.

But he was only faintly troubled, like a man hearing ill of a new acquaintance and not quite believing it. Whatever the trouble in the basin, it was not his quarrel, and the pay was unheard-of.

"They'll accept my freight," he declared. "I set it up with Santa Fe to run a spur to La Cinta if Great Southern bucked me. So I'm covered there. Now, then," he said severely, "is that why you were trying to dump my train in the river? Because you were afraid I'd go broke?"

A train whistle piped wetly. They heard the hiss-and-chuff of pistons, and then Jim's private car came in view around the turn on the hillside above them, green panels gleaming, brass and glass shining, the other cars and the locomotive following. Anders tossed the crowbar aside, stood up and rubbed his palms together. His shirt was glued to his shoulders with sweat. "Sometime," he told Jim, "you'll have to straighten out a tie for me, Jim."

"Any time," Jim said agreeably, "I'll straighten you out too, if you ever need it. Miss Hester, I'd be honored to have you as a guest on my train. Your uncle's waiting for me at his siding? Good. Chet can drive your buggy back, can't he?"

Hester said she would be pleased to accept.

CHAPTER 3

SHE SAID her uncle was working cattle at the siding two miles south. "They're road-branding some steers this morning. He's sending them up to Albuquerque."

As the train started, Jim told the girl about his private car. It had once belonged to Collis P. Huntington, of the Central Pacific. "I think he traded it in on something with a fireplace," he said. She smiled, and he was relieved that she could unbend. She would come around, a pretty girl like Hester. She was quiet, yet with something special about her—her own sort of strength. Jim drew his chair close and patted her hand.

"Now, Miss Hester, tell me the truth. Do you honestly think my railroad will hurt your uncle?"

"I think a railroad which failed might kill him. If you know as much about the basin as you say, you must know it's his life. I think the biggest thing he prays for every night is a railroad. He thinks it would be the flame to light the wick of the lamp for Magdalena Basin. After that, Chicago would be just a suburb of Divide, New Mexico. That's our county seat. He wouldn't let them name it Travisville."

Jim frowned down the tracks. "I still don't understand why you're so convinced I'm going to fail."

The breeze, warm as child's hand, ruffled Hester's red-gold hair. "Somehow," she said, "I have the feeling your intentions toward our valley are not quite honorable. Your letters to Uncle Cam have been so glib. And my goodness—a man of your age to be promoting a railroad all by himself!"

15

"I've got backers." Jim admitted. "Naturally I had to sell stock."

"Ah," she said. "Stock! Is there any limit to how much any one hayseed can buy?"

Jim stared fixedly across the basin. "I hope I find your uncle more friendly than you, ma'am."

Hester patted his hand, as he patted hers. "I'm sure you'll find him pathetically friendly. If this is a confidence game, you'll have enough confidence left over to sell ten hogsheads of hair restorer."

They were approaching another trestle. A hillside sloped down to it. Along the stream were high, airy cottonwoods. Just short of the bank, where the rails ended, a siding pulled away left. There were corrals here and a loading chute. A sign, glistening with new paint, identified Travis Siding. Bawling Angus steers raised a dust, heavy as nutmeg, among the trees. In the main corral some cowboys were branding steers while an old man with a tallyboard on his knees watched from the top rail. Another man sat beside him twirling a short length of rope. The engineer blew the whistle smartly. Horses reared and the cattle began to mill. The men jumped down, the older one staring at the string of cattle cars between Jim's car and the tender.

"Holy Smokes, boys!" he shouted. "Cattle cars!"

They started down the hill. The old man limped on a stiff leg. He looked as stubborn and tough as an old badger. He wore his hat on the back of his head and his chin was like a saddlehorn. His General Lee beard wanted grooming. Jim dropped to the ground and went to meet him.

Cameron Travis gripped Jim's hand and peered acutely into his eyes. It reminded Jim of having a bullseye lantern thrust into his face on a dark night. He felt like blinking. But at once Travis' features relaxed.

"You're Harlan, eh?"

"Jim fits better. Cameron Travis?"

"Call me Cam. Everybody in New Mexico calls me Cam." The old man removed his hat, resettled it, and suddenly remembering the man at his side, put his hand on his friend's arm. "This here," he said, "is Day Clevis, neighbor man."

Clevis, the neighbor, was a tall, hard-fleshed man with something Spanish about his dark features and gray-black hair. The top half of his left ear was missing. He had a shy back-country manner and when he shook hands with Jim his grip was flabby. But there was no softness in his face, and he wore a diamond as big as a pea in his lodge ring.

He said he was real pleased to meet Jim, and what were the cattle cars for?

"I thought Cam might have a few cattle to ship," Jim said. "They can go back with the train crew. Sort of a sample."

Travis started to speak but held it. His eyes looked as though he had been reading poetry. After a while he said gently, "Well, that's real nice of you, Mr. Harlan. Real nice."

On the railroad car, Hester fanned dust from her face with a folded newspaper. "Mr. Harlan, will that slide-rule of yours tell us how to load cattle with a rotten chute?"

Jim smiled. "Plenty of two-by's on the flatcar."

Cameron Travis regarded his niece sternly. But Day Clevis touched his arm, scratched his head, and said, "Say, uh. If you got any extra space, Cam—this being the first trip—kind of an honor, do you see—"

"Shoot, you can have a whole carful for yourself," Travis said. "This fella," he smiled at Jim, "was my biggest stockholder in the old railroad. Reckon you lost nigh as much as I did, didn't you, Day?"

Clevis resettled his Stetson over his face. He could hardly see out from under it. "Right around there," he said.

Travis turned to bawl at some cowboys in the corral. "Tear down that old chute and fix up a new one! One of you ride out and tell Bill Holly we won't need the chuckwagon. Jim—" he smiled, showing pipe-eroded teeth—"I'll give you four bits for a tour through your car. I declare that's the prettiest thing I ever saw!"

While they were going through the car, Chet Anders drove in. Jim could see him talking to the men who were rebuilding the loading chute. Then the foreman strolled over to the tracks and joined them in Jim's office. Jim was showing Travis his rolls of plans and the big map on the wall.

"These are the same plans you registered yourself," Jim said. "I'll follow your route from this point right on to Silver City."

"They ought to be good," Travis said. "Clarence Dykes was my chief engineer. He was with U.P."

"Dykes!" Jim exclaimed. "Is that the man who registered a coalfield in the San Pedros last year?"

Travis chuckled. "That's the man. I expect he'll be richer than French cooking after your railroad reaches him."

Jim smiled. It was pleasant to think of an old man becoming rich that way. Then he heard Hester's voice, and he flinched.

"How did you know about Dykes' coal, Mr. Harlan?"

Jim gazed at her thoughtfully. Travis said a gruff word to his niece and the moment was awkward.

"I want to make something clear," Jim said. "I picked this area for my railroad after I'd explored freight possibilities—not before. Now, it seems to me that you and Chet have the idea I'm some sort of confidence man. If that's what you're trying to say, please say it."

Hester faced him, abashed but determined. "Yes, I guess that is what I'm trying to say. I think you *are* some sort of confidence man. You aren't my idea of a railroad man at all."

"Hester, for Lord's sake!" Cam Travis exploded. He stared at her in anger and embarrassment.

Color invaded Hester's face. "I'm sorry, Uncle Cam. I didn't want trouble, but if Mr. Harlan insists I'll speak my mind. Did you ever hear of a man his age building a railroad with his own funds? Could you even dream of building a railroad without exploring the entire route first?"

Travis' eyes watered as his face began to redden. Chet Anders scratched a match on the wall, leaving a yellow streak. "I've seen carpenters take more pains with a hen coop than this fella takes with a railroad, Mr. Travis."

Travis' anger broke. "Go back to the cattle, Chet! Do the work you're paid to."

The foreman's mouth hardened. His hand carried his cigarette to his lips. Then he threw the cigarette down and passed from the car. Cam Travis squared off to his niece like a bulldog.

"Now, then, Missy, let's have that speech about railroad building!"

Hester looked cornered, but did not retreat. "It's just that I love you and Aunt Carrie very much, Uncle Cam. I won't see you hurt if I can help it. It seems as if the slickers sell gold bricks in the cities, and railroads in the country. Have you forgotten the Cuchillo Valley Railroad? People bought stock in it, but all that was ever built was a fortune for the promoter. And the Oak Creek Railroad! Why, the company took the town's bonds and bypassed Oak Creek by five miles!''

''My route is a matter of record,'' Jim said.

''What about your capital? Is it a matter of record? Or will you go broke after you hit the mountains—so the basin will have a total of two failures against it, and no legitimate railroad will ever touch it?''

''I'm not going broke,'' Jim said. ''I can tap all the capital I'll ever need.'' He looked at Day Clevis.

''And have you all the right-of-ways you'll ever need?'' Hester smiled.

''No,'' Jim said. ''That's why I'm here.''

''When do you plan to talk to Tom Sorrell?'' Hester asied.

Jim faltered. ''Tom Sorrell?''

''*Senator* Sorrell, that brass-knuckle statesman who wrecked my uncle's railroad ten years ago, and will probably wreck yours. He led Great Southern's fight against our Short Line at the capitol. How can you even pretend to build a railroad when you haven't got your right-of-ways?''

Think big, Jim! Sullivan used to say, when they were in a corner. Bluff, browbeat, or buy your way out of it.

Jim heard himself laughing with all the easy confidence in the world. ''Yes, ma'am, I know about Tom Sorrell. The things I could tell you about him! The stunts he pulled in the senate that he'd like to forget! I've got letterpress copies of some letters he wrote. If Tom Sorrell so much as drops ashes on my carpet, I'll pull the skies down on him. It's like they say, Miss Hester: Never was a horse that couldn't be rode.''

''Another saying I like is: Never a man that couldn't be throwed.'' Hester smiled winsomely. But suddenly her uncle seized her by the wrist and pulled her around.

''Hester, you'll look mighty unladylike if I have to upend you over my knee! Exactly what is it you're asking of Jim?''

"References," Hester said. "Statements of assets. Names and locations of other railroads he's built. Whether they're operating now or have fallen into ruins."

"I've had all those. You've read them in Jim's letters."

"But so vague, Uncle Cam! The Canela and El Vado Railroad. The Chihuahua-Boquillas! And names of men we never heard of as his backers. I mean—well, gracious, if you were shipping five thousand steers to him, you'd investigate his references first, wouldn't you?"

The color seeped out of Cam Travis' face. His eyes crackled blacker. "Go to the buggy," he said. "You will not insult our guest any further. When Jim and I are finished talking, I'll ask you and Chet to witness some papers."

Hester's palms pressed against her hips and she shook her head. "No, Uncle Cam. It's my business as much as yours."

Jim chuckled. He must break this up quickly. "If it will make the lady feel better, we can finish later."

The girl brought all her anger to him, now, her eyes all pupil, her lips tense. "What *would* make the lady feel better," she flared, "would be for you to pull your train out of here and never come back! Now, I mean this, Mr. Harlan—you may get permission to cross my uncle's land, but you'll never cross *my* land!"

Jim smiled. "Excuse me, but I'm not interested in your land."

"Oh, but you are! Half of Muleshoe Ranch is mine. My father and Uncle Cam were partners until my parents died. We're on my land right now."

CHAPTER 4

JIM KNEW he must have looked sick.

Cam Travis did not dispute it. Day Clevis rubbed his neck in embarrassment and said he thought he would be going. "Just rode over to smell train smoke again," he said. "I'll see you at the next passin', Jim." Without a glance at Hester he walked from the car.

There was a crumbling sensation in Jim. He was cold with anger and disgust. He said to Travis, "I wish you'd told me you didn't control this land. I've gone to a lot of expense on the assumption that you did."

Travis lifted his hand toward Jim but still faced his niece. "Have you any idea what you're doing to me, Hester?".

"Mr. Harlan," Hester appealed, "won't you go up and talk to Chet? I'd like to talk to my uncle alone."

As Jim went out, he patted her hand. "You're a real nice girl, Miss Hester, but you ought to leave business to the men."

At the corral, two men were hammering spikes into two-by-twelves while another tended branding irons in a fire fuming in the middle of the main corral. A cowboy dropped a gray Muleshoe iron in the coals and took out a frosty-red iron. Chet Anders was leaning against his horse, chewing a match while he regarded the car with malevolence.

"The old billy-goat," he said. "Five-foot-six of whiskers and brag. Quit him in a minute."

He drove his fist against his palm and Jim looked at the big, square-cut silver ring he wore and knew what Anders was thinking.

He was hitting Travis in the face with that ring. He decided to try to mend fences.

"What's wrong with us, Chet? Travis throws you out, and the girl throws me. Let's get up a poker game."

"Only man's game left, now that knife fightin's illegal," Anders said. He winked. "Unless you count railroad swindles."

"Get it out of your head that this is a swindle!"

Anders' teeth rolled the match. "Don't make a bit of difference to me how you skin the old 'coon. I've tried to teach him ranching for two years. He's ranchin' just the way my grand-daddy ranched. All sweat and no brains."

"I don't care how your grand-daddy ranched. But keep your mouth shut about my being a swindler."

Smiling to himself, Anders struck the chewed match and watched it burn. "You know how come I savvy you? Because I've known dozens of men just like you. I used to be a guard in the pen at Santa Fe. Every third man looked like a banker. *You* look like a banker, Jim! Young banker. You look a little bit like a prisoner who made this ring for me. Made it out of a 'dobe dollar. Maybe I'll be standing guard over you some day, after I get fired from here. Maybe you'll make a 'dobe dollar ring for extra rations."

Jim took a handful of Anders' shirt. The taste of copper was in his mouth. "Don't you know when a man means something?"

Anders smiled. "Maybe you think I care."

Jim knew the Travises would watch it, and old Travis would get the wrong idea about him. He would think that a man who got into fights so easily could not be much of a railroad builder. He pushed Anders away.

"It's coming, Chet," he said, "It's coming!"

Down the hill, Travis called, "Harlan! Will you come here?"

Jim started back. He heard the ramrod say, "Stick it in him and break it off, Jim. Don't make a bit of difference to me."

Hester was coming toward the buggy. She was weeping. She started to say something, but her voice broke. Jim took her hand in both of his and said gently, "Miss Hester, I'm sorry. I didn't aim to make trouble. But I don't like people to make me trouble, either."

"You don't care about anything," Hester said brokenly, "so long as you drive ahead. You don't care for anyone but yourself."

"Now, Miss Hester—"

She bit her lip until she could control it.

"You're to move your car off my land by tomorrow night. If you don't, I won't be responsible for what happens. Maybe I'll burn it!"

Jim laughed. "If you do, I'll cut that pretty hair off and plait myself a bridle."

Raising her skirts, Hester went up the hill to Anders. Jim's expression soured. There was no great difference between this railroad and the ones he had worked on in Mexico. He and Sullivan had built them for government subsidies. If the railroad worked, it surprised them and they shook hands on it. Whether it ran or not, nobody claimed he was being mistreated. And there was always the danger of being executed by a new government, which more or less justified the profits.

But Hester, with her wailing over right and wrong, made it sound as though he meant to lay rails on the bones of men he murdered. And this talk of Sorrell and Great Southern, . . . You're a sly one, Senator, he thought. Grind all the axes you want, but not on my stone. I'll build this railroad, and I never heard of you, and it will work.

Cam Travis was waiting by the tracks. His hands were thrust into his hip pockets and he gazed up the hill at Hester and Anders.

"Jim," he said. "I'm sorry this had to happen. Some of Muleshoe does happen to be my niece's land. But I've operated it since my brother died and I'm charged with operating it until she's twenty-five. So don't worry about her."

The girl stood by the corral with her head lowered while Anders spoke to her. The foreman was holding her hand.

"She told me she'd burn my car if I didn't move it," Jim said. "Who's going to worry about that?"

Travis brushed his beard with his knuckles. "Hester will get herself a hiding if she keeps on talking long enough. What she told me was that I've got no right to make a contract for her that will be binding after she's twenty-five. Hogwash! I'll shearcrop it all into black-eyed peas if I want."

"Maybe she's right," Jim said.

"Hogwash," Travis said again. His eyes watched his niece instead of Jim, and Jim thought he sounded uncertain. "We'll have to go to town now to get those papers witnessed. Better make it tomorrow. I'm going up to Lopez Meadow today to buy a Mexican's chili crop. You'll have to go to Divide anyhow, so I'll meet you at the hotel. Divide's four miles, the county seat. I had them save you a room at the Home Ranch Hotel. Town's alive with drummers and beef buyers. I brought you a saddle horse.''

It seemed to Jim that Travis didn't have his mind on what he was saying. Hester's buggy moved away on a tilted wagon road which led toward distant bluffs on the east, and Travis watched her. "You know, Jim," he said with a smile, "I have as much regard for a good woman as I have for a good horse. In their place, they're fine. But I don't take business advice from a horse, so why should I take it from a woman?''

"Steer by that and you'll never go wrong." Jim chuckled.

They walked up the hill. Jim adjusted the stirrups of the long-legged bay which Travis had brought for him. He heard Travis speak to Chet Anders. "We'll need another twenty steers from the Atarque pasture, Chet. Start them up as soon as you can. I'm going up to Jacinto's.''

Anders drew on the cigarette and exhaled the smoke. Silently he looked at the rancher. "Did you hear me?" Travis asked.

"I heard you. I'm quitting," Anders said.

"Quitting! Maybe *I* didn't hear *you,*" Travis said.

"If this is Miss Hester's land," said Anders, "It ain't your call to roust her off it.''

"There's plenty of good ex-ramrods about Divide," Travis said loftily.

"There's one more now," Anders said.

Travis tugged a clasp purse from his pocket and counted out some gold and silver. "This cleans us up," he said. He tossed it to Anders, but Anders let it fall to the earth. Anders spat on the money.

"*Now* we're cleaned up," Anders said.

Hester had driven a mile when she heard the horsemen behind her. She glanced back, hoping it was her uncle, and saw Chet Anders. She was driving down a mesa which sloped into a valley green with poplars. Where the mesa fell off, she stopped in the mounded ruins of an Indian camp.

With the breeze against her face, she gazed down the basin.

Irrigated farms followed the streams, and the high land, the mesas, were peppered with junipers and fine graze. She loved it all. But Jim Harlan, with his cardboard railroad, could destroy it—bankrupting half the farmers and ranchers in the basin with his worthless stock.

She turned as Anders dismounted. He had a deep, powerful body, short and strong, and a blunt masculinity. His face was grave.

"I'm sorry, Miss Hester. I did my best to rattle that railroader. But I'll stand by you anyhow," He coughed. "I've quit your uncle," he said.

"Oh, but he needs you, Chet! Oh, I think it's a shame—"

"I've been ready to quit for a long time. That old man's got his ideas about ranching, and I've got mine."

"I can see the good results of a lot of his ideas from here," Hester protested.

Anders shrugged. "Oh, sure, I've heard he built this basin single-handed. But now he ought to bring his ranch up to date before it gets away from him. He's raising a risky breed of cattle when the money's all in whitefaces. And there's others things—letting old timers camp on you. Opening haystacks on the weather end so the rain comes in and sours them." He snorted. "Sometimes," he said, "I have to line the men up and ask how many are carrying pliers or a hammer in their chaps pockets."

The girl smiled. "Are we hiring cowboys or carpenters?"

"Suppose a cowboy comes across a spring box caving in. He can fix it, if he's got a hammer. Save a day's work later on."

"May I see your hammer, Chet?" Hester asked soberly.

Anders drew a small claw hammer from his chaps' pocket. Then he grinned. "I've tried to tell your uncle that, but he takes to advice like a hog takes to table manners."

Hester saw a new dimension in Chet. He was one of those very ambitious men with a mind full of ideas but no chance to test them.

"Did you have any other job in mind when you quit?"

"I'm not a rash man," he drawled. "I figured you'd need a ramrod, if it comes to a split."

"I don't really think it will come to a split. But maybe there is something you can do for me. Do you remember the squatters you moved off Iron Creek two years ago?"

That was when Anders had come to the ranch. He had been hired because her uncle needed a roughneck foreman. Travis had always treated squatters well, but the ones on Iron Creek had been merely establishing rights they meant to sell. When his foreman failed to roust them, Cameron Travis found a new man in Albuquerque— Chet Anders. In a week the squatters were gone.

"Sure, I recollect them."

"I was wondering if you could handle Mr. Jim Harlan the way you handled them?"

Anders rubbed his nose. "The prescription might be different, but I reckon I could use the same spoon. Fellas like Harlan make a lot of noise, but call their bluff and they back right out. Unless they think they're tougher than you are."

"Does Harlan think he's tougher?"

"I don't think he is. If I whip him and he comes back for more, I'll show him a carbine."

"Absolutely not. I want no gunplay, Chet."

"Then there won't be any gunplay. Unless he starts it."

"See that he doesn't."

Anders ran a hand along her horse's back. "Afterwards, why not set up headquarters at old Fort Quanah, on Iron Creek?"

She hung back. "I really think my uncle will come around, Chet. And if he doesn't, I don't know for sure that I can do anything about it."

Anders' face was charged with force. "Yes, but he can't make a perpetual contract for you! You said so yourself."

Pride and anger had carried Hester this far. But she did not wear rebellion easily. She had been raised to believe that women should not meddle in business. Shaking her head, she told the foreman:

"I think if you can't frighten Harlan out, we'll have to forget it."

"Now, that's nonsense, Miss Hester! Acre for acre, there's no better range in the Territory. It ain't right to let it be—be tore apart by this fellow." Chet's gaze held Hester's sternly.

"We'll talk about it again," the girl said. "Why don't you ride over and have a talk with Mr. Harlan? He's probably on his way to Divide right now. Oh, and Chet—you'd better let me take your Colt."

Anders hesitated. Then he grinned and handed her the gun. He roughed his pony around while he mounted. The half-trained bronc circled once and Anders quirted it over the head with his rein-ends. He had a lazy, assured power which caused Hester to be slightly alarmed for Jim Harlan. She was afraid of what she had set in motion. Harlan was much slighter than Chet, and if he stood up to him he would take a beating. And though he had it coming, she had an unpleasant recollection of fights she had glimpsed in cowtown streets—men with torn shirts and bloody faces ripping at each other.

She pressed her lips together and drove toward the ranch.

CHAPTER 5

JIM HARLAN placed a few things in a carpetbag and started for Divide on the horse Cameron Travis had provided. It was a beautiful rosewood bay, probably the pick of Cam Travis' riding string. He rode down the creek and crossed where it was wide and shallow. Trout darted over the brown cobbles, and Jim wished for the Mexican village where he and Drew Sullivan had holed up between administrations. Trout fishing, Spanish wines, and conversation: what more did a man require?

Well, a girl, perhaps. But not a girl like Hester Travis. Not a girl with a man's will. Not a little girl who scarcely outweighed a saddle, whose waist you yearned to squeeze between your hands, a pretty and engaging girl, but too smart. He remembered the blueness of her eyes. He recalled how large her pupils were when she turned on him. He liked the way she held her tears until the last. Most women came primed with tears as a Colt was loaded with bullets.

A quarter-mile ahead, his eyes were caught by a rider who lunged up from the creek. As he topped out he glanced back toward Jim. Then he halted beside an oak. Jim recognized Chet Anders by his striped jersey. He was puzzled for a moment. Then the thought struck him: By heaven, he's working for Hester now!

He felt irritated and uneasy, thinking that Anders might have planted the whole thing in the girl's mind. Anders was blunt, but there was a slyness in him, too. Jim could see him more easily in his former role as a guard in the territorial prison than he could as a ramrod. He had known other men like Chet Anders—ambitious but unsuccessful, because they could not steer around their own failings.

As Jim rode up, he squared his pony off to Anders'. Anders' sleeves were rolled. He had thick, muscular arms. He wore his hat cockily and his knee was hooked around the saddle-horn.

"Big hurry, Jim?" he asked.

"Keeping busy," Jim said.

"You keep busy doing the wrong things, Jim."

"What am I doing wrong now?"

"Riding in the wrong direction. Out is north."

"Fast work, Chet. Working for Hester now?"

Anders nodded. "She sent me to tell you—get going."

Jim kept thinking. There must be a way to handle this bull. He was not afraid of Anders, but how could he play the empire builder in Divide with two black eyes and a split lip?

"You're picking a loser, Chet," he said sadly.

Anders made his fist and gazed affectionately at it. "There's my winner. Ain't let me down yet." His heavy silver ring was like the jagged end of a stick.

"Are you going to take that ring off, or will I have to even things up with a rock?" Jim demanded.

Anders drew off the ring. "You've got more guts than most phonies, Jim. But I'm going to break you right in two. Don't you know that? Right—in—two!"

Jim dismounted. They confronted each other on the loose, gravely trail. Anders' shoulders had the long slope of great power. He was obviously stronger than Jim, but the way you used your strength was as important as the strength itself. Jim kept studying him.

"We ought to make this worthwhile," he said. "I'll bet my horse and outfit against yours."

"What do you want to do? You'd have to pay Travis three hundred dollars for that bay."

"I just don't like borrowing horses. After I win yours, I'll give Travis his back."

"If you win my horse, Jim, you'll earn it. You won't straddle it for a month." He chuckled. "Better take off your coat. You're going to need all the swingin' room you can get."

"That's right," Jim said. He stripped the coat from his left shoulder, and as he had expected, Chet Anders stepped in and fired a thundering right. Jim slipped the coat back on his shoulder, but he was an instant late: The blow struck him high on the forehead. Pain flashed against his eyes. He fell back as Anders charged with the headlong power of a wild pig. Hard-bodied, he collided with Jim. Jim slugged him twice, once in the face, once in the belly. It was like hitting a boar, too; there was no give to Anders. He was solid and fast and he loved to fight.

The collision knocked Jim flat on his back. Anders drove his boot into Jim's hip with all his strength. Jim gasped. He thought his hip was broken, but struggled to his knees. Anders charged in high and hard, but Jim caught him around the legs and the foreman crashed on top of him. He began savagely gouging at Jim's groin with his knees.

So it's going to be like this, Jim thought. Anders had learned his ethics in back alleys. Jim slugged him under the ear and Anders' vicious struggling slackened. It encouraged Jim to know he could be hurt. He slugged the foreman again and scrambled up, but Anders followed him in a lunge, his face distorted.

Jim unbuckled his belt as he dodged back. He was faster than Anders. He sidestepped and ducked and the foreman could not get his hands on him. Jim flipped the belt from its loops and took it by the tongue, swinging the heavy buckle around his head in a whistling circle. Anders blinked as he watched the shining arc of the buckle. Then he swore and tried to come in under it. Jim slammed the buckle against his ear and Anders shouted a curse. He kept driving forward. Jim stung him on the side of the head, but Anders suddenly seized the belt with both hands and yanked at it. At once Jim released it. Anders shuffled back as he went off balance, and Jim went on lightly, his fist going back to full cock. Then he threw his fist with full power into Anders' face. He felt the sweet shock of the blow all the way to his shoulder.

Anders was on his knees, the flesh of his chin split open. With blood dripping onto his shirt, he looked too big, too tough, to be hurt. But he was hurt. His head would clear in a moment, so Jim stood over him and taunted him.

"Come on, you big bucket of muscles! You were going to break me in half."

Anders came to his feet, but staggered when he was upright. He swung a wild blow and Jim went under it. Then Jim fired straight at his chin again. It was light hitting a tree. As Anders stumbled back, Jim went with him, his face grim. He caught Anders with a round-house blow to the ear, threw another which rocked his head back, and at last there was the clean punch like a cannonball, hard and definite and final.

Gazing down at the foreman, Jim breathed deeply. Anders lay on his back with his mouth open, blood already coagulating on his chin. Then Jim looked down at himself. He was filthy, but there was little blood on him. He would show a bruise on his forehead, and a cut at the outer corner of one eye. He walked to the creek and washed his hands. He held them in the water until his knuckles ceased bleeding.

He went back. *I wonder if he'll try it again? If he'd ever landed one of those he'd have knocked my head off.* Well, Anders would not try it again today, because he would be afoot. That was why Jim had wanted his horse.

He mounted, picked up the reins of the foreman's pony, and started for Divide.

CHAPTER 6

LEADING ANDERS' HORSE, Harlan came upon a good wagon road. He knew this was the main road from La Cinta to Divide because it was paralleled by a line of telegraph poles and carried the ruts of heavy travel. The power of Chet Anders' fist still rang in his head like the waning vibrations of a bell. The foreman was as solid and strong as a draft horse, and Jim felt fortunate to have gotten off with a cut beside the eye, a few bruises, and a sleeve torn from his coat. Nevertheless, he decided, he could not ride into Divide looking like an itinerant horse breaker.

Having put some distance between himself and Anders, he began looking for water. The road had climbed, but now it began to work down through sparse tangles of brush. The road cut back and forth over crumbling ledges of rimrock. Just before he reached the bottom, he saw some ruined buildings under a bluff. They were of adobe, roofless, and laid out about a square. Beyond the buildings a stream moved glisteningly under an arch of cottonwoods. Jim supposed it was an old Army post, which, following the fate of old Army posts, now served as occasional roundup headquarters and lodging for drifters and coyotes. He could see a corral made of small branches and barbed wire. Black fire rings could be discerned among prairie dog holes on the parade, and some old hides lay near the only building with a roof.

Jim rode through the fort, stopped at the stream to let the horse drink, and pulled off his coat and shirt. There were red bruises on his chest where Anders' fists had smashed home. He looked at himself in the stream. Then he scooped up a double handful of water and washed. He combed his hair and pulled on his shirt. Without buttoning or tucking it in, he picked up his coat and began examining it.

"Damn," he sighed. The sleeve was ripped out at the shoulder. And besides, it hurt him to see anything with a lot of good wear left in it spoiled like this. That vagrant thrift in his profligate life was the only legacy his father had left him. Like an old fever, it seldom recurred. Harlan Sr.'s spectacular failure had convinced Jim that in order to survive, you had to start fast, hit hard, and never slow down. All his life Jim's father had fumbled along, worrying about honesty, morality and thrift. Now there was left of him only the sad memory of a bearded man with a bitter tongue, who had stood in an out-of-plumb ranch house doorway, having failed for the final time, and told his son:

"It don't matter how you git there, Jim—just git there!"

It was sour advice, but through the mind of Drew Sullivan, the man he had gone partners with in Mexican railroad building, he had distilled it into something fine and useful, Golden whiskey from sour mash. You had to remember where the drift fence ran between honesty and dishonesty, that was all. And if you had to sin, make your sins count. It was a workable, happy-go-lucky philosophy. Its only inconvenience was that occasionally, like Sullivan, its practitioners blundered before firing squads. But when they did, they did not go down on their knees and beg. The preachers told you they would, but in practice it was usually the small, strait-laced man whose code failed to support him in his last hour.

A pony which had stood very quietly in the trees across the stream moved toward the graveled bank, and Jim straightened quickly. His hand touched his thigh, but his Colt was wrapped in a newspaper in his carpetbag. He saw then that the rider was a young woman. Her hair was dark and she wore a grey delaine riding dress. As she rode the horse into the water, she sat her side saddle daintily, watching the pony's feet grope for footing. It was Sorrell's wife, Lovena. Hastily Jim began tucking his shirt tail in, but just then she looked up and smiled at him.

"I'm sorry, Mr. Harlan," she said. "I didn't mean to eavesdrop. I'd stopped here to water my horse and you frightened me away."

"Come on over," Jim called. "Myself, I just stopped to run up a new coat, but now I can't find my needle."

As Jim put his hands up to help her down, she glanced into his face with surprise. "I do believe you've been in a fight, Mr. Harlan!"

Jim swung her down. "You could call it that." She was very small, with a slender waist and a wonderful figure. She must spend more money on clothes than a cavalry regiment spent on dress blues, he thought. There were just the right tucks and ribbons in her gowns and she used very little jewelry. In the lobe of each ear, a tiny diamond sparkled. She wore a necklace of yellow gold with a small filigreed pendant. I'd like to give her a bracelet, Jim thought breathlessly. I'd like to see it on her wrist. But this gift-giving, he knew, was a very bad symptom, and he set his mind against it.

"But what happened?" she asked him.

"I guess you know Chet Anders?"

She winced. "How many did it take to subdue him?"

"Just me. All of me, that is."

Lovena turned from him, raised her skirt and tore a piece of cloth from one of her petticoats. "At least I can stop that cut from bleeding."

She dampened the cloth in the creek and Jim sat on a broken wall while she pressed the cold pad against his eye. With his other eye he peered into her face. He knew she was aware of his scrutiny because she smiled a little. He remembered every tiny feature of her face, the dark brown of her eyes, the cocoa tinge of her skin, the way her mouth dimpled when she smiled.

He had known a share of girls, but she was someone special, a girl with whom a man could not be impersonal. She was very conscious of being a woman and glad about it. And Jim remembered with a small pang something he had begun to forget—how he used to be unable to sleep after seeing the Sorrells in Santa Fe, because he would rehearse everything he had said to Lovena and everything she had said to him. Her slightest remark seemed to glisten with special meaning, and after a time he admitted to himself that he was in love with her. He knew he would have to cut her out of his mind, yet there she was. She meant more to him than a married woman should. He had old-fashioned ideas about marriage, and he was glad when the Santa Fe work ended.

"Aren't you going to tell me about the fight?" she said.

"Do you know Cam Travis' niece?" Jim asked.

"Don't tell me you've been fighting over Hester!"

"No, but she's got it into her head that I'm some sort of confidence man. Travis will straighten her out. In the meantime, she's hired Anders away from him. I expect he was just making his muscles for her."

"What did you call what you were doing?"

"Business," Jim said crisply. "Strictly business. She wasn't even there to see it."

Lovena took the cloth away and inspected his eye. "I think perhaps you're going to be all right. Just don't get into any more fights over Hester Travis."

"That's good advice. And thanks for the surgery. One of these days I'll do a favor for you."

"Next week, perhaps?" Lovena said.

He knew by the way she spoke that she was serious. "Next week?" he said. "Today. What is it?"

"Build me a siding to our ranch," she said.

He gazed at her. "Are you serious?"

"Serious? I'm absolutely determined. I want a siding. I want it as soon as you can build it. I want it to start at Red Hill and run right up to our corrals."

Jim laughed. "Maybe you'd better open that cut again. I don't think I can pay the price."

She pouted. "You're an ingrate, Jim Harlan! I'll never tend your wounds again."

"But a siding!" Jim said. "What does a girl your size want with a siding?"

"How can you park a private railroad car without one?"

"Have you got a private car?"

"No, but I'm going to as soon as I have a siding," she told him.

He smiled. "And after I build the siding, then I give you the car—right?"

"Wrong," she said. "My father will give me the car. He knows how lonely I get because Tom's away so much. If there were a fit way of traveling, I could go along. Most often there isn't, and when you get there there's nowhere to stay but a drummer's hotel next door to a slaughter house. So father wrote last month that as soon as you've got started he wants to give me a private car so I can go along! The company has this old car and he says he'll have it refitted and send it down.''

Jim rubbed his jaw. He wanted to do it for her, and he knew why he wanted to do it. The old infatuation was in him stronger than ever.

"Lovena, I don't know." He frowned. "If you were a rancher dying to ship his first load of cattle, and I knocked off work to build a siding, how would you feel about me? You wouldn't be very enthusiastic, would you?''

She looked away, her face disconsolate. "I'd feel just as I do now. Because you won't build my railroad either.''

Against all his motives of caution, he decided to risk it. "I'll make you a bargain," he said finally. "If Tom approves it, I'll build it.''

Her face lighted. "Promise?''

"As soon as I reach a turnoff.''

She sighed. "You're very nice. And after all, I wouldn't ask you to do it without proper thanks.''

She went on tiptoe to slip her hands behind his head and kiss him on the lips. It startled him, and then it was warm and wonderful, and as exciting as a breath of perfume in a dark room. Suddenly he put his arms around her. Though she tried to pull back, he made the kiss last until they were both breathless. At last he let her draw back. Flushed, her hair slightly disarranged, she stood small and open-mouthed before him.

"Why, Jim Harlan! You know I didn't mean anything like that!''

"I'm going to give you some advice, then," he told her. "Don't ever do it again. Some people you can play post-office with. Some you can't. As far as you're concerned, I'm one you can't.''

"Are you such a bear?" she asked.

In Jim's heart there was a sad sort of joy. "Don't you know what I'm talking about?" he asked her. "I'd always heard women could spot a conquest two rooms away.''

She glanced away as if embarrassed, but he saw the small tucks of pleasure at the corners of her mouth. "You're teasing me.''

"I wish I were. I'd give a lot to be teasing, but I'm not.''

"Jim, dear," she said, "you don't love me. You're just—''

"Just in love," he said, "and not very happy about it.''

She looked into his eyes, and he saw something she had not shown him before, something sober and disturbing. "Is it my problem," he asked, "or is it ours?"

She turned her back to him and looked down at her clenched hands, and Jim pulled her back against him. After a moment she leaned her head against his shoulder. "I don't know," she said. "I've tried not to think about it ever since Santa Fe."

Jim brushed his lips against her hair and gazed across the range. "Did you marry Tom Sorrell because you loved him?"

"I don't know," she said. "I let my family convince me I loved him. You might say I was put up as collateral on this railroad project. Tom had been courting me for three years, and I think he let father know he'd block this railroad project if he didn't get some definite encouragement from me. So they began encouraging me to encourage him."

Jim's tone hardened. "Why did you let them?"

"Don't scold me, Jim. It's bad enough without being scolded. I couldn't help myself. And everyone told me I was marrying so well."

It was quiet and Jim's thoughts were long and realistic.

"This is a pretty big country, Lovena. I wonder if we could keep enough of it between us so that we won't see each other again?"

"Would you like that?"

"Would I like having a broken leg set? No, but I'd know it had to be done."

Lovena went to sit on the wall overlooking the river. She smoothed his torn coat on her lap. "I think that would be a very painful way to set this particular broken leg," she said.

"I know this much," Jim said. "The longer it's put off, the worse it's going to get. Whatever's going to happen had better start happening pretty soon."

She turned back a revers of her gown and drew out a needle with some thread wound about it. "I can't set broken legs," she said, "but perhaps I can do some good for this coat." She smiled at him without much happiness. He watched her as she began to stitch the torn shoulder.

"It might make some difference," he said, "if you told me

whether or not you're in love with me. If you're not, everything's simple. I walk out.''

"Don't you think a thing is easier to bear, sometimes, if you don't name it?''

He chuckled. "That's known as looking the facts squarely in the oack of the neck.''

Then he saw her eyes go beyond him, past the fort and up the slope, and saw her eyes widen. "Jim,'' she said, "look! There's someone watching us.''

CHAPTER 7

JIM GLANCED AROUND. The sun shone crisply on the cottonwoods. There was no one in the fort and he saw no one on the hillside. "I don't see anyone."

"Up on the bluff."

His eyes settled quickly on the horseman. "Yes."

"I think it's Dick Spurlock, our foreman. Is he riding a grulla?"

"Yes. That's why I didn't see him. He blends into the brush."

"And that's no accident, either. Dick's like an Apache scout. I don't know how he gets any work done when Tom's away, for watching me. Don't stare at him. Perhaps he didn't see—"

Jim heard the pony's hoofs on the road. Lovena finished with the coat. "Try it on," she said.

Jim pulled the coat on. He saw the rider come down the slope from the road into the fort. He rode erect and precisely, as straight-legged as though he were walking. He handled the pony like a loaded Colt. It moved affectedly, and Jim thought no working cowboy had a right to spend so much time teaching a horse so much foolishness. Spurlock would be as efficient as a sergeant major Jim reasoned, but the cowboys would stop talking when he opened the bunkhouse door. He decided that even before he could see Spurlock's face, and when he saw his face he was sure of it.

Spurlock raised his gloved hand to them, smiling. He carried his other glove tucked under his gunbelt. He was slender and dark-haired, heavily freckled, and he looked as hard as a rawhide rope.

"Don't we get around, though, Dick!" Lovena greeted.

"My job," Spurlock said. He gazed at Jim, then.

"This is Jim Harlan," Lovena said. "You've heard Tom speak of him."

Spurlock said, "Glad to know you," but he did not offer his hand. You could not ask for a more efficient way of telling a man you had seen him kissing your employer's wife.

"Does your job bring you over here?" Lovena asked.

"It does when you ride over," Spurlock said. "You're counted an Easterner until you've had five years' experience in New Mexico. Easterners wander off and get in trouble."

"You're a good foreman." Lovena smiled and tapped his arm. "If I were your Sunday school teacher, I'd give you a New Testament for faithfulness."

Spurlock smiled. Jim saw him begin to soften. A stain of jealousy began spreading through him. Lovena was smiling at Jim now.

"Mr. Harlan, I don't know how much good I've done that coat of yours, but I am glad I came across you in your trouble. Do drop in on us, won't you?"

"Right soon," Jim said. "And thanks for the help."

Spurlock dismounted and picked up the reins of Lovena's pony. His narrow hips turned like those of a Mexican dancer. As he saw Jim's extra horse, he glanced around. "Ain't that Chet Anders' horse?"

Jim said, "It was. I won it on a bet."

"What kind a bet?"

"He bet I couldn't, and I bet I could," Jim told him.

Lovena spoke quickly. "Chet started a fight with him. Jim had to whip him."

Spurlock grinned with half his mouth. "You whipped Anders? I've seen tougher men accomplish less." He led Lovena's horse up. Jim got the impression he would never laugh out loud, unless he laughed at someone. Spurlock boosted Lovena onto the saddle and she glanced down archly as she arranged her skirt. "Easterner!" she said. She laughed softly. She did not look at Jim again.

Jim watched them cross the creek and disappear behind the cottonwoods. Then he smacked his palm with his fist. He wished you could take a pill to get over a girl, the way you got over a headache. The foreman was in love with her. He could see that plainer than tracks in mud. And he was in love with her, but he couldn't be sure she loved him. Maybe she just needed admirers. Maybe she collected them.

He walked to his horse and mounted Travis' rosewood bay. If he got lost in his railroad, he should be able to forget about her. But he was quite sure he would not.

Taking a small trunk, Hester Travis left Muleshoe ranch that afternoon.

There had been a tearful scene with Aunt Carrie, which almost broke Hester's will to force the hand of Jim Harlan. But she felt that she could make a better stand if she got out from under her uncle's thumb, by moving to town for a few days. Her aunt wept and scolded, but Hester continued packing. Carrie Travis was an Alabama lady of mild and sweet deportment who thought a girl must always bend to masculine breezes, and then achieve her desires by cleverness. Her legacy to Hester, whom she had raised since the age of nine, was a satin sachet-bag full of small female stratagems:

A girl must never appear to hunger for anything. Neither must she be the only giver in a match. Married, she must willingly assume the white woman's burden on the frontier, the effortless operation of a household with or without servants, the fight to keep the gentle things from being lost in sweat and dust. And the only weapon she could legitimately raise was patience.

"But how could you use patience with a—a freight engine of a man like Harlan?" Hester demanded. "Once he gets up momentum, nothing can stop him. He'll have our own friends on his side!"

"Perhaps that's where they belong, dear."

"Not if he means to fleece them. I just can't believe any honest man would rush into railroad building like this. And apparently without partners, or the fortune it will take. And so sure of himself! So utterly, utterly sure!"

"A man who intends building a railroad should be sure of himself."

"And I'm just as sure that he *isn't* going to build a railroad," Hester said. "So I'm going to stay at Fowler's hotel until things are settled. I want to talk to Francis McKenna about my rights." McKenna was the family lawyer. She felt she could depend on him not to open a case purely for fees.

"You know, dear," Carrie Travis said, "there are various ways to accomplish things. Do you remember the new rooms I wanted to build, and Cameron said I couldn't? But when he was in Chicago one time I had them built. He ordered me to my room when he came back. But the next day he let me out and gave me the earrings he'd brought back, wrapped in a poem he'd written me."

Hester's lip trembled. "Locked you in your room! Why must we always be the ones to give in and be locked up?"

Her aunt smiled. "Who's to say who gave in? I got the rooms I wanted, and on top of it a poem."

"But if I don't do something about Jim Harlan now, Uncle Cam will sign with him tomorrow!" She told her aunt about commissioning Chet Anders to frighten Harlan out. There was a chill quiet. Hester felt like a hussy who had set herself as the prize in a street fight. "Don't you see— -force is the only thing he understands," she argued.

"Force," Carrie Travis declared, "is a word young ladies should use only with reference to corset strings."

Hester asked Bill Holly, the range foreman, to carry her small rawhide trunk to the buggy. Holly was a tough, baldheaded man with bulging eyes and a ridge down his head like the spine of a razorback hog. He insisted on driving Hester to town. They drove off with her trunk bouncing in the back of the buggy. Not far from the ranch they came upon Chet Anders limping back to the ranch. The foreman stood stolidly in the road while they stared at him. His face had been brutally mauled. His chin was split open and the skin about his right eye was turning blue. Anders' big shoulders sloped with exhaustion.

"Man!" Bill Holly breathed.

"Chet! *What* under the *sun!*" Hester exclaimed.

Anders said with his teeth locked, "I misfigured him."

Hester was suddenly ashamed and discouraged. "We both misfigured him. I'm sorry I led you into it, Chet. Under the circumstances—"

Anders stubbornly raised his hand. His spurs, buckled to his belt, jangled. "I never said he was tough. I said I misfigured him. We've just started with Mr. Harlan." He frowned at the jagged face of the ring he wore. "He asked me to take my ring off, and while I was twisting it off he hit me."

"He do that?" Holly frowned. He looked dubious.

Hester gasped. "Why, I think that's outrageous! It's not better than shooting a man in the back."

"But now that we know how he plays, we'll be ready for him." He spoke thickly. "I'll buy a crowbait from your uncle and load out my gear tonight. Tomorrow morning I'll clean Harlan's plow."

"No, Chet," Hester said. "Fighting won't do any good now. I thought perhaps we could frighten him. But unless Francis McKenna says I have the right to fight, my little war is over."

Anders' frustration boiled into his eyes. "My little war's just started. Harlan's leaving. I'll take my Colt, now, if you're carrying it."

Hester's heart squeezed and then seemed to expand until it choked her. "There'll be no gun-carrying, Chet!"

Anders' eyes, the bleached color of old denim, were intractable. "Won't, eh?" he said. "There's a carbine in my blankets."

As he started on, Hester laid the buggy whip against his chest. "You'll not carry a gun to town, do you hear?"

The foreman angrily snapped the whip from her hand. Then he set his jaws, reversed the whip and handed it back to her. He seemed to take himself in charge. He turned his head to expectorate and there was blood in the spittle.

"All right," he agreed. "But we know he don't bluff. He'll blow this range six miles high with his phoney stock, but if it ain't worth fighting over, why that's your say, Miss Hester."

He walked on, limping, his tied spurs jingling. Hester was sorry for him. He had quit a job in her behalf, and now, unless she went ahead with her threat to block Jim Harlan, he was jobless.

"Old Chet's all heated up, ain't he?" Bill Holly said.

"Yes. Drive on, Bill," Hester said. Straight and tense, she peered ahead and they drove on.

The afternoon stage from La Cinta approached as they were nearing Divide in its cloud of dusty trees. Hester heard the brush cry of the driver's copper horn. Billy pulled into the bar-pit to let it pass. Every outside seat was occupied. The men all lifted their hats and called greetings to Hester. Drummers, cattle-buyers and drifters: Autumn sifted them into the basin as it shook the brittle leaves from the cottonwoods. She wondered whether there would be a room for her at the Home Ranch Hotel.

They drove into Divide while lamps were going up behind dusty windows and supper fires filled the streets with smoke. The evening was cool, the street crowded. Divide had grown from a little Mexican Plaza. Its building stood about the square like a military post. There was a Mexican church and a county courthouse with twin horse troughs, as ugly as iron bathtubs. Most of the buildings were two-story adobes with wooden galleries forming an arcade above the walks.

At Evans' hide-and-wool house, stiff cowhides were being thrown down from a freight wagon.

They stopped before the Home Ranch Hotel. The gallery was crowded with men who stared at her openly. As Holly unloaded the trunk, Joe Fowler, the proprietor, came out. A fleshy, red-faced man, he had a napkin tucked into his collar.

"Well, Miss Hester!" he said. "Are we going to have the pleasure of your company?"

"Can you put me up, Joe? Such a crowd!"

"Always, Miss Hester, always," Fowler said with his uneasy red-faced heartiness. He moistened his fingertips and slicked down the thin reddish hair of his temples. He took her small trunk from Bill Holly and hoisted it to his shoulder.

"I'll stable the rig and be at Bill and Emma's if you want me," Holly told Hester.

Hester and Joe Fowler crossed the porch.

"By the way—a good friend of yours is staying with me," he said. "A Mr. James Harlan."

"Did Harlan say he was a friend of mine?"

Fowler had to swivel his entire torso to look at her. "No, ma'am, but since he's doing business with you uncle, I figured—"

Hester did not comment. As Fowler selected a key, a man came into the door of the dining room. He was lithe and tall, and his skin was dark with weathering. He smiled and made Hester a slight bow. He wore a corduroy coat with a black string tie, and he was carrying a napkin in his hand. It was Jim Harlan. There was a bruise on his cheek and a very small cut beside his eye. It seemed incredible that he had butchered Chet Anders with his bare fists.

Fowler started to introduce them, but Harlan said, "I've already had the honor, Joe. Miss Hester, can you give me one good reason why you shouldn't be my guest for dinner?"

"I could give several," Hester said. But as she thought about it, she added, "However, it might be less awkward than staring across the dining room at each other. Thank you. Will you wait ten minutes?"

"I've been waiting all my life," Jim said.

Hester washed the dust from her hands and face and changed into a pale green gown. She was excited. In the mirror, her pupils looked very large, and she had what Uncle Cam called the weak trembles. It was too bad Harlan could not be fat and unpleasant, but of course confidence men never were. Nevertheless, she reminded herself severely, he probably was dishonest. When she entered the barny dining room she had added green earrings to point up the red in her gold hair and make her skin look fairer.

As Harlan seated her, she gave him a cool glance. "I must say you look better than Chet did."

"Chet had bad luck," Harlan said sympathetically.

"Is that what you call hitting a man while he takes his ring off?"

"Is that what he told you?" Harlan chuckled. "Well, if it makes him feel any better, I'll let it ride. Have you really moved out on your uncle?"

"You saw my trunk,"

"It wasn't a very big trunk,"

"I can get very mad on a very small trunk."

"You got pretty mad today on no trunk at all," Harlan agreed. He studied her curiously. "What do you plan to do now? Chet must have told you I don't bluff. What's next?"

"I'm going to stay in town until I've settled the question of whether Uncle Cam has any right to do business with you. If he can legally sign for me, I can't fight you and the basin will just have to take its chances. But if my lawyer say he can't—"

She faltered. Lean and brown, he looked attentive without being in the least disturbed. To him, she must seem just a woman making boasts she could not back up. He probably considered her as ludicrous as a woman throwing a ball. He had the kind of face you might see across the poker table, cool-eyed and implacable, and she yearned to upset him. "Of course," she said loftily, "my withdrawing still wouldn't help you with Tom Sorrell."

"I told you I could handle Sorrell."

"And I still don't believe you," said Hester. "I think you see yourself buying him a drink and joshing him into cooperating with you. You don't know Tom Sorrell!"

"Tell me about him."

What could she tell? That he had killed Uncle Cam's railroad? He knew that. That he had the financial manners of a cougar at dinner? He probably wouldn't be impressed by that.

Suddenly she remembered.

"He killed a man once!"

"Once," Harlan said, "generally does it. What was the trouble?"

"The man was a squatter. There was some trouble, and Sorrell killed him."

"I'm not a squatter," Harlan said, "and I've got the papers I told you about."

That stung Hester to sarcasm. "If you can sign him up, I'll be there to applaud."

Harlan's eyes quickened. She felt she had made a tactical blunder. "What if I sign him up tomorrow?" he asked.

"You won't."

"But will you pull in your pretty little horns if I do and let your uncle go ahead with me?"

"Oh, now, wait—"

"Wait nothing! The only reason you've opposed me, I gather, is because you think I'm a bungler. You don't really believe I'm dishonest, do you?"

Her gaze wavered. How could you tell a man to his face that you thought him a criminal? And the point was, she suddenly did not want to believe him a criminal. Through some feminine back-flip of the intellect she was becoming fond of him.

"Well, all right, if you can show me Tom Sorrell's signature on a right-of-way."

Harlan relaxed. "I was wrong about you, Miss Hester. You're the most sensible girl I've ever known."

"And what girl wants to be called sensible?" she said archly. "I even use a little rouge sometimes."

"You shouldn't. You don't need it."

Hester dropped her napkin on the red-and-white cloth. She saw that he considered the fight finished. She hoped it was, but in case he failed to swing Tom Sorrell it would be well to have kept things on a last-names basis.

"I'm really quite tired," she told him. "Shall we say eleven o'clock tomorrow, in the lobby?"

Harlan escorted her to the door of her room.

"Sixteen!" he said, reading the number on her door. "There's a coincidence. I'm right next door to you!"

"How nice," she said.

"You know," Harlan told her, "you've got a real pretty voice, Miss Hester. But I didn't notice it until you began saying the right things. Sometime I'd like to hear you sing."

As she closed the door, she had the impression that he was less gay than he wanted her to believe. He was a man with a worry. I wonder if it's a girl somewhere, she reflected. The thought dampened her. Why, it struck her, he might even be married! And for some time she was unable to compose her mind for sleep.

CHAPTER 8

THE BUNKHOUSE was empty when Chet Anders rode in. All the men were out on the fall work—rounding up, repping, branding calves missed on the spring gather. Anders' Colt lay on his bed, where Hester had left it. He holstered it and began throwing things in his canvas warbag—socks, razor, a striped town shirt, some journals of animal husbandry. He saw a large oil stain on one book and he sniffed it. Liniment. Stinking horse liniment! He slung it into the sack. Then his angry mood swelled and with his head lowered he stared about the long earth-floored room. Sweat and horse liniment! The stink of them passed for air in bunkhouses. Caved-in cots, alarm clocks, antelope prongs, candle stubs—these passed for furniture. He had lived in bunkhouses so long he thought of them as prisons.

Even the guards' dormitory at Santa Fe had been better. Ramrodding prisoners had been little different from chousing cattle. He might have stayed, but a church group had toured the prison one day and convinced the governor that the inmates were not being treated like gentlemen. So a lot of the guards had been fired.

Preachers foamed and shook over the future. *Where will you spend eternity?* they asked. Anders knew. Cowboys spent eternity in trashy hells that smelled of liniment.

He had hoped, when he came here, that Travis would be progressive and the ranch would prosper and he might have a chance to buy in, or at least keep a brand. But Travis merely listened to his suggestions, patted him on the shoulder and said, "We'll think about it some day."

Slumped on the cot, Anders tugged off his boots. The exertion made his ribs ache. The taste of bile rose in him. Standing, he clenched both fists and with his bare feet widely set he stabbed at a vision of Harlan's grinning face. *Get up, you big bucket of muscles!* Harlan had taunted him. Anders' fist smashed his palm. He had tried a trick on Harlan, but Harlan had seen it before. But there were some other tricks they had used in a room without windows at Santa Fe, and Chet Anders remembered the sick eyes of the men they carried out. There was dancing eagerness in him to get Harlan in a corner and give him the edge of a hand on the bridge of his nose, and see the gut-shot look swim into his eyes when the pain kept coming and the knee found his groin.

Anders slumped on the cot again. He had come face to face with a growing fear, the only fear he could not trap in a corner—the fear of failure. What happened that a man's plans fell apart like a rotten hide? He was strong and not afraid of work. But he had never had a nickel, so he could not test his own ideas about ranching.

On a long shelf pegged to a pebbly wall, an alarm clock chipped away at eternity. Time—the cornmeal running out of the torn bag. And Harlan, this Fancy Dan railroad builder from Mexico, had torn the hole bigger for him. Every job you quit put you back that much farther. The slack came and it was the new punchers who got fired. Anders was thirty-three, now.

Through with packing, he walked to the corral and caught out a saddle horse and a pack mule. He saddled both animals, put the blanket roll and heavy gear on the mule, and tied the warbag behind his saddle. He didn't trust a gray mule. They would always roll on their load. Damn a gray mule. He rode past the woodpile and kitchen garden at the rear of the main house, down the side of the square adobe building, and around to a wall with an arched gate in the center. He opened the gate and walked through a patio garden of yellowing rose bushes to the porch. It was kept screened with mosquito bar most of the year. A Mexican girl came at his knock.

"Get the boss-lady," Anders said.

Carrie Travis appeared. She was a rather aimless little woman with a tired, sweet face. She put her hand to her bosom when she saw his beaten face. "Why, Chet! Whatever in the world!"

"Horse rolled on me," Anders said. "I'm quitting, Mrs. Travis.

This is for the horse and mule.'' She looked at the money he handed her.

"I don't understand. Did Mr. Travis ask you to leave?'' Old women's faces were as irritating as the faces of ewes. "He'll tell you about it,'' Anders said. "Here's forty dollars. It's all I've got.''

"Mr. Travis certainly wouldn't send a man away without a horse after two years' service,'' Carrie Travis declared. "You keep your money, Chet. Are you sure you have to leave?''

"Yes, ma'am.'' Anders set the double-eagles on the plastered sill. "I don't want to hang for horse stealing, though. Well—adios, Mrs. Travis.''

"Chet, I wish you'd let me make you some tea. You don't look well at all.''

Tea. I'll be damned, he thought. "I might just take a jolt of whiskey,'' he said baldly.

"You know Mr. Travis doesn't permit liquor on the ranch.''

"I know—strong drink, strong language, or cards. Adios, Mrs. Travis.'' He jogged out of the ranch yard.

Tea and a free horse, he thought. I'd like to see this place two years after the old man dies and Carrie's been running it. A financial report, to Mrs. Travis, was when you turned the sugar bowl upside down and some money fell out. Two years of her management and nothing would fall out but ants.

No, he thought, she wouldn't even try it. Either she'd sell out or Hester would take the reins. He gazed over the long dun-and-purple sweep of range with its bowls of early shadow. It was impossible to see all of Travis' land, the sections he owned outright, the sections he leased, the forest leases. Suddenly he was filled with hatred for Jim Harlan. He had always liked Hester and he thought she liked him. Maybe he would have married her and been ramrodding all of this himself some day, if Harlan had not come along.

He took his eyes from the broken grasslands. It was well not to look covetously at things you could not afford. This was sound bunkhouse wisdom.

Anders struck the county road and turned north toward La Cinta. It occurred to him that he would be passing Jacinto Chaves' farm, where Travis had gone to buy chilis. He hoped it would rain and all the chilis he bought would mildew in the field. The road climbed, the shadows sprawled. Anders was in the hills now, with two hours to ride before he came out on the high mesa. The road teetered along a hillside which slid into a canyon. A copper telegraph wire slung along beside the road on spindly poles.

Up the road, Anders heard the hollow clack of hoofs. He hoped it was not old Travis, but it probably was. Anders pulled his pony in and the mule rammed into the back of it. Anders angrily struck it over the head with the end of the lead rope. Cameron Travis came into view around a turn on the steep hillside. His bearded old general's face looked startled as he discovered the foreman.

"Well, you didn't stay around long," Travis said curtly. "I thought you were going to join the ex-ramrod's club in Divide."

"Did you?" Anders' raw temper began to smart.

"Wait a minute!" Travis said. He was looking at Chet's horse. He leaned aside to glance at the mule. "Those are my animals," he said.

"Were your animals," said Anders. "I paid the old woman for them."

"What old woman?" Travis' brow flushed with displeasure.

"Your old woman. Old Carrie," Anders said boldly.

"Get off that horse and unload the mule," Travis snapped.

"You go to the devil," Anders drawled. "I said I'd paid for them."

"How much?"

"Forty dollars." Anders recalled that he had no receipt.

Travis stared into his eyes. "Where's the bill of sale?"

"I didn't ask for one."

"Get off the horse," Travis repeated.

Anders said, "Go to hell."

Travis kicked his pony and rode in close beside Anders. He dismounted and Anders watched his long, thin fingers grope under the fender for the D-ring and latigo. He began uncinching the saddle. Anders' temper exploded like a cartridge in a campfire. He put his hand in the rancher's face and savagely shoved him away.

"You old goat!" he shouted. "You want it good? You want it so you'll remember?" He turned the ring on his hand to bring its jagged face up.

Travis charged him. Anders clubbed down at his face and the ring on his hand ripped a cut across Travis' eyebrow. The blood was thin and red and unaccountably it enraged Anders and threw the rough-lock from his reason. As Travis reached up to drag him from the saddle, Chet drew his Colt. He flipped it and caught it by the barrel. Then he chopped viciously at the rancher's head. Stunned, Travis fell back against his horse and the foreman hacked at him as he tried to protect his head with his raised hands. All the time Anders was crowding his pony into Travis', crushing him between them.

Suddenly Travis' pony lost its footing on the narrow road, and fell. Travis fell beside it among the rocks. They began to roll downhill in a gray cloud of rock-dust.

Anders watched numbly. The old man and the horse rolled and sprawled all the way to the bottom of the canyon. There, in the clotted shadows, they came to rest. Anders saw the horse try to rise, then fall back. He could not see Cameron Travis.

Anders sat there with his lips moving and his mind absolutely motionless. He could not believe it. I just killed Cameron Travis he thought, and kept staring down the hill. They'll lynch me, he thought. Everybody liked him. They won't believe he attacked me. Or did he attack me? Did I start it myself? He said I'd stolen the horses. Damned liar. But who's going to believe me over him?

Suddenly it seemed to Anders that he must ride like a demon to La Cinta and hop a train. No! he thought desperately. That would really hang it on me. I'd have to keep traveling forever. Maybe he isn't dead, he thought. He started down the hill, the pack mule bungling along behind him.

Halfway down a light turned on in his brain. If Travis were dead, Hester would take over. Mrs. Travis would manage the rose bushes and the meals, but Hester would run things. You might say that the foreman who helped her run things would eventually become her husband. At least he would be the real power on Muleshoe, and if he had a lot of ideas stored up, he would make a name for himself.

Anders found Travis near the horse, as dead as anyone could wish. He gazed down dumbly at Travis. Well, how can they prove anything? Nobody saw me come up here. Nobody knew where I was going. If I go to Divide, bold as brass, who'd even suspect me? In twenty-four hours I'll be working for Hester.

He scratched his ear. He began to grin. Then he realized the horse was squealing in agony. Anders thought indecisively, I can't leave it like that. It'll suffer all night. But he couldn't leave a bullet in it, either.

He dismounted and opened his clasp-knife. He sat on the horse's head and groped for the big vein in its neck. He made a small, quick cut and felt the hot wash of blood on his hands and sleeve. His hand leaped away. He started to wipe it on his pants but realized what he would be doing. He took a handful of sand and dry-washed until he felt clean. In the dark he could see that his sleeve was soaked with blood. Have to wash it. No, get rid of it.

For a moment he stood there looking up at the sky, greenish with the young evening. It was quiet. He grew tranquil. He rolled a cigarette, listened for sounds, and heard a deer on the road. He listened to its hard-hoofed patter as it smelled the blood. Then it stopped.

Shock was running out of Anders' big body. He used to ridicule faint-hearted prisoners. *You gotta be tough, boy.* Tough in mind and body. Anders took pride in his own toughness. He could stand a lot of physical pain and he did not rattle easily.

He mounted his pony and looked down at the shadowed lump old Travis made on the ground. It did not disturb him. His hand went to his tender, fist-mauled face and he winced. *Okay, Mr. Harlan,* he thought. *Now we're ready to talk business.*

CHAPTER 9

AT LA CINTA that morning, Tom Sorrell had loaded his cattle into railroad cars. All but one of the riders who had come with him boarded the train to feed and water the stock. Sorrell and the other puncher started home. On the way, the rancher sent him to see what was doing in the late calvy herd. Now, in a rusty sunset, Sorrell approached old Jacinto Chavez' goat ranch in the foothills, and thought about Jim Harlan.

It was odd that he should feel a wry affection for Harlan. He guessed he just liked a man who dared to bluff. But Jim Harlan had to learn when to quit bluffing. If he did not learn easy, he would learn hard, like his friend Sullivan, who had died before a firing squad in Mexico.

Passing the Mexican's hut, Sorrell smelled chili and cheese. His jaws ached with hunger. If Chavez were one of his own Mexicans, he would stay for a bite, maybe spread his blankets with him tonight. How shocked Lovena's people in Cincinnati would be! The son-in-law of Rawlings of Great Southern sleeping in a dirt-floored Mexican hut!

"People of quality." Sorrell recalled with a fuming of anger how Mart Rawlings, Lovena's father, had used the term on him—that same devastating phrase with which he had struck down Jim Harlan this morning. He was courting Lovena then—a second-rate suitor, of course, because nothing west of Cincinnati was really worth a damn—and once to impress them he had described a ranch he had recently added to his property.

"That ranch cost me seventeen thousand dollars, Mr. Rawlings!"

Rawlings spoke to the fuming tip of his cigar. "People of quality, you know, do not talk of what they own, Mr. Sorrell."

Even a roughneck Western cattleman whose suits came out of the wrong catalogue could comprehend that. Sorrell was tolerated in the Rawlings home, on his frequent trips East, because he had handled Great Southern's New Mexico business for years. Rawlings pretended friendship just as Sorrell did. He did it for money; Sorrell did it for Lovena.

He loved Lovena as only a man past forty could love a girl of eighteen—desperately and uncertainly and with a hang-dog heart. Sorrell made himself over to win her. He fashioned himself into a clipped poodle though he had run all his life with wolfhounds.

He qualified at last by cornering Rawlings on the Magdalena Basin railroad.

Sorrell said he wasn't sure he could arrange it. Santa Fe had requested a charter, he said. He said he might even build the road himself. It would be a gem of a paying road . . .

And so he married Lovena on her twenty-first birthday.

A couple of miles below Chavez' farm, Sorrell was startled by the sound of a small avalanche directly ahead. He saw a horse crashing down a hillside. Then he saw a man rolling in the dust. He loped ahead.

He came to a turn where dust hung in the air. Below, a rider was cautiously descending the slope. Sorrell recognized the burly shape of Chet Anders. He started to shout. But then he noticed the roll behind Anders' saddle. Where would Anders be traveling at round-up time? It seemed to Tom Sorrell that this whole thing had a left-hand thread. He led his horse out of sight and knelt in the backbrush beside the road, watching Anders reach the bottom of the canyon.

Anders did nothing for a full minute but stand by his horse. He seemed to listen for whatever scrap of sound was in the air. Sorrell saw him look up the canyon and then down. Sorrell crouched lower in the brush. He saw Anders move quickly, kneeling beside the injured man for a few minutes, then rising and walking to the downed horse. The rancher wished it were a half-hour earlier; the shadows hung thick as cedar smoke. At last he observed the

Muleshoe cowboy mount his horse again, take a last, long look
about, and ride down the canyon.

Slowly Tom Sorrell stood up. He could feel his heart thumping
high in his breast. As yet he did not give a name to what he had
witnessed. He walked to his horse and drew his carbine. In the late
twilight he walked down the slope. He found the man lying there
near the horse, struck a match and cupped it near the bruised
features of an old man with a beard and wispy gray hair lying over
his brow. Cam Travis! Sorrell dropped the match. He felt cold,
shocked, and shamefully exultant.

Anders! he thought. *The copper-bottomed fool! How did he think
he could get away with it?*

He lighted a small branch of juniper and thrust it in the sand while
he examined the rancher's body. But the only blood was on his
head. Once he had seen a man run over by a freight wagon. He had
looked just about like Travis.

Sorrell carried the branch over and inspected the horse. It was
curious that it should have died. Men died easy but horses died hard.
A lake of blood had collected under its head. Sorrell looked for the
knife cut, found it, and stood up marveling at the compassion of a
murderer who could not bear to see a horse suffer.

The rancher climbed the slope hurriedly. Before he reached the
top, the meaning of Travis' death began to deepen. Plainly, Chavez
had to be told to collect some cowboys and move Travis to town.
But what about Anders? Sorrell felt as though he had just filled a
royal flush. He held Anders in his hand like the red ace.

He started for Jacinto's cabin. Maybe there was no rush to inform
on Anders. He could say, later, that he had not been sure; that he
wanted to follow his tracks; something like that. In the meantime, if
Jim Harlan got out of hand, he could trump him with Anders. He
would give Anders his choice: Be a trump, or a long-necked
cowboy at the end of a rope.

Sorrell shouted and the old Mexican came from his hut. "Travis
is dead," Sorrell said. "Horse ran off the road."

Jacinto went to his knees, crossed himself and began to pray.
"Get off your knees," the rancher said curtly. "Ride to Travis'
Saguache camp and get some men to tote him out. *Andale!*"

The moon was rising when Sorrell opened the last Missouri gate and jogged up the dark wedge of pasture which ended in his corrals. Dick Spurlock, his foreman, came from the bunkhouse, swinging a lantern. Spurlock helped him unsaddle and gave a report on everything which had happened that day.

"Old Travis ain't dug out that rattleweed yet," he said. "Going to be poisoning your cows one of these days."

"Set fire to it as soon as it's dry enough," Sorrell said.

"Travis will raise hell," the foreman said.

"Not so it'll fret us any," Sorrell said. He did not want to say anything about Travis to Spurlock. "Where's Mrs. Sorrell?"

"In the parlor, I reckon. Been looking for you."

"Did you see Harlan up there at the fort?" Sorrell asked. "I saw his tracks."

Spurlock's thin, freckled features held steady; a little too steady, Sorrell though. "I passed some words with him," Spurlock said.

"Was Mrs. Sorrell with you?"

"No, sir."

Sorrell's eyes pried steadily at his foreman's. "Who rode to the ranch with you, then? I saw where two horses crossed the creek."

"I reckon one of the boys rode in after I did." Spurlock picked up the lantern.

"You're lying, Dick," Sorrell said. "What's the matter? You didn't forget you were a foreman, did you?"

Spurlock reddened. "No, sir. Mrs. Sorrell asked me not to say she'd been riding alone, because you don't like her to."

Sorrell grinned. "That's what I thought. But you don't have to police my family for me, Dick. If Mrs. Sorrell gets hurt, she won't need hurting twice."

The strain left the foreman's freckled face. "All right. But you know them Easterners! Mount a horse with a bunch of wildflowers in their hand, and the horse boogers. Pick up a piece of rope and it's a sand-rattler."

"You're talking about Easterners. Mrs. Sorrell became a Westerner when she married me. It's like a foreigner getting citizenship by marriage. She's a real New Mexican now."

He walked stiffly toward the big ranch house. Old cottonwoods with clusters of mistletoe in their branches shaded it. The house was like a long blockhouse with a shake-roofed gallery and identical wings running back from the front. The rear was open, but a high wall sheltered the enclosed patio.

In the hide-rugged parlor with its smoky beams, Sorrell sat on the raised hearth to remove his spurs. He dropped his Stetson on the floor and laid the spurs in the crown of it. While he was pouring himself a drink, Lovena entered.

"Tom! I didn't hear you come in." She wore a close-fitting green gown and her dark hair was done in a neat chignon. With her rich coloring she looked almost Latin. She was as dainty as a chatelaine watch, and he went toward her, hungry for her. Lovena smiled. "Oh—I'll tell Criseda you're here."

She went to the door of the dining room and called to one of the maids. Then she returned to take his hat and spurs to a table. He watched her, a flicker of resentment in him. How many times had he aimed a kiss at her lips and found her cheek?

"New dress," he commented. "I believe you must sew all night."

"Only to kill time when you're away." Smiling, she held out the full skirts.

"I like it," he said. "I mean to order a glass bell to put over you." Sorrell poured himself a second drink, impatient to feel the liquor cutting away his fatigue.

"At least you'd know where I was without setting your foreman to follow me."

Sorrell felt the thorn in her banter. "His idea, not mine. I told him tonight he doesn't have to police you for me. You won't get hurt, and after all I trust you."

"I should hope so!"

He sat down and cocked his leg across his knee. "How was he, by the way?"

"Who?" She was fussing with some flowers in a vase.

"Jim Harlan."

"Why, he was fine." Quickly she turned. "Tom, guess what! He's going to build our siding first thing!"

"What the hell do we want with a siding?" Sorrell snapped. "I'm sorry, Lovena, but—a siding!"

Lovena's manner chilled. "If we're going to quarrel over this silly railroad, I wish you'd stop the whole business."

"But why tip off everyone that I'm helping Harlan?"

She told him about the private car, warming again. He listened with stolid anger, his features swarthy and set. "If you wanted a private car, why didn't you tell me?"

"Tom," she laughed, "private cars cost a lot of money."

Sorrell said, "I'm giving you enough to eat, I hope? And you don't really have to make your own clothes, you know."

Lovena crossed the room. "We don't seem to have much to agree on tonight. I'm going to my room."

"No, you aren't," Sorrell said. He finished his drink, and taking her by the arm he placed her in a chair. "We're going to talk about some of those things we don't agree on."

The girl's eyes were dark. "Don't you think it's vulgar to argue while you're drinking?"

"Vulgar!" he retorted. "Do you always have to throw an etiquette book at me? Maybe I should buy myself some pumps and hire a French dancing master."

She bit her lip. He knew she was going to cry and tasted a mean pleasure. "Excuse my bad manners," he said. "You see, I climbed out of the wrong side of the Mississippi River this morning. I'm just a roughneck Western cattleman. I've tried, but the fact is your people still think of me as a hog rancher."

"Tom, that's simply not true!"

"And I'll tell you something else!"

He knew he was slightly drunk, but the process of getting these things off his mind exhilarated him. "If your people thought I was as rich as they are, I could drink beer out of a boot and they'd take theirs the same way!"

"If you have so little regard for them," Lovena asked quietly, "why do you care what they think?"

"I don't. Not one damned bit. But I'm going to show them they don't know anything about being big, with their Eastern ideas of bigness. Big! The biggest peanut in the world is still a peanut. Iron deer on the lawn and French cooking! Listen, Lovena. Tom Sorrell is going to be so damned big your father will trail me around to pick up my old diamonds."

"Really?" she said.

"Really. I'm going to own this whole basin one day, and that will only be the start. I'll have the finest herd of whitefaces and my own strain of registered stock. I'll make my pile out of coal and railroads, but I'll sink every nickel of it in cattle.''

Young and frightened, but taking courage from her pride, she sat calmly with her hands in her lap, palm-up. ''Then all you need, I gather, is a railroad and a coal mine.''

''Yes, ma'am.'' Sorrell walked a few strides away and turned with his hands in his pockets, grinning. ''And both are coming up. The Magdalena-Silver City Railroad and a coal mine right beside the tracks.''

''I didn't know you were interested in Harlan's road.''

''Oh, yes. I'm taking it over after he goes broke.''

''Is he going broke?''

''Harlan will do almost anything for a price. My price for going broke will beat your father's price for not going broke. He's going to the block, and I'm going to buy him out.''

''Now you own a railroad,'' she said. ''What about the coal mine?''

''Clarence Dykes owns the finest coal field outside of the East right here in the San Pedros. Dykes will get tired of waiting after Harlan goes broke and I'll buy him out. I had the field cruised last year. My geologist figured that ten New Orleans chippies spending money twenty-four hours a day couldn't put a dent in the revenue.''

''Do you have to talk that way?'' Lovena asked him.

He saw the fear in her eyes. A drunken hunger to hurt her ignited in him. He looked at her bare shoulders and throat until her hand strayed to the bosom of her gown. He walked to her and grasped her shoulders with his hands.

''Yes, ma'am,'' he said, ''I do have to talk like this. Because I'm drunk. Drunk and talking good sense.''

''Please take your hands off me,'' she said.

He did not. ''It would be all right for Harlan to do it, wouldn't it?'' he said.

''Why do you say that? Why Jim Harlan?''

''Because you were with him at Fort Quanah today.''

Her eyes wavered. ''It simply happened that I was doing a watercolor of the fort when he came along. You don't need to be jealous. He's simply a capable and pleasant man whom you introduced me to yourself."

"Is he capable and pleasant when he takes you like this?"

Sorrell bent and kissed her roughly on the lips. She struggled. He straightened, chuckling. But then he saw her face. She looked like a little girl frightened by a stranger. It cut him like a saber, for what he saw in her eyes was hatred and fear. He knew it had been there all the time; he had merely uncovered it. He felt desperate and torn, because love was the first thing he had ever wanted that he could not seize.

"You have no right to do this to me," she said brokenly.

Sorrell moved back as she stood up. His craziness was going flat. He wished he had drunk less. His voice roughened with emotion. "Lovena—don't you see why I'm doing this? It's for you, not me! I want you to be proud to be Mrs. Tom Sorrell."

"Isn't it curious," she said, "how we find excuses for what we mean to do anyway? I've watched you eye old Mr. Dykes' property ever since he found coal on it. You have a greed and a vanity like a bonfire. They eat everything you feed them, and then you grab at something else."

She moved to the door with a crisp rustling of petticoats. She was so young, so dainty, so lost to him, that it hurt him to look at her. "It's plain you need a vacation from me, Tom. I'm going East."

Sorrell spoke with slow weight. "You will not go one foot off this ranch, Lovena. This is your home. I'm not going to give you up to Jim Harlan or some purebred Cincinnati loafer."

After she left, Sorrell drifted into the patio. The night was crisp, shot with stars. A frog belly-flopped into the little pond. He wished he had not said it about Harlan kissing her. But he wondered if it were true. Maybe he could get it out of Spurlock. He paced through the patio to the door of his bedroom and lighted a Mexican petticoat lamp on the clothes press. He looked at his coats. He pulled out an old gray-and-black striped coat he had not worn since he began courting Lovena. He put in on and found he had donned a mood with it, his old mood of rough-and-rediness, his pride in his trade, his hard-handed self-confidence. Rough as burlap, plainly cut, it was a good cowtown coat he had drunk in and worked in.

He was done with aping his wife's father! Time for her to learn a husband was not the same thing as a father. If he could not win her love, he would hold her respect, and by heaven her faithfulness too!

He stuffed some things in a brown valise. There was a lot to be done in Divide and he wanted to be on hand in the morning when they brought Travis' body in. He wanted to see how Chet Anders behaved if he were around. If he were not around, it would be important to find him.

CHAPTER 10

As JIM HARLAN prepared for bed in the Home Ranch Hotel, where Travis had saved him a room, there came a tap at his door.

"Mr. Harlan?" Joe Fowler, the hotel keeper, stood holding a steaming pitcher of water.

"Reckoned you might like a jug of hot water, Jim." Jim had insisted on the first-name basis.

"Why, thanks much."

As Jim took the pitcher, Fowler put his hands in his pockets, pulled them out again, and said, "Say, uh. I was down to the Gold Exchange with Mr. Dykes tonight. He came in late from his ranch; been staying with me lately while he waited for you. So, well, we were talking to Chet Anders—"

"Chet in town too?"

"Came in just a bit ago, looking mighty sorry. And he—well—"

"Joe," Jim said seriously, laying his hand on the hotel man's sleeve, "do I have to get out of town?"

Fowler's blond eyebrows lifted. "How'd you know that?"

Jim began to laugh. "I knew that when I looked at Chet today after I knocked him out. I don't know what you heard, but it was a good, clean fight. As I was looking at him, I told myself, 'By tonight he'll be drunk and telling people to tell me I've got twenty-four hours to get out of town.' I never built a railroad yet that some hothead didn't give me twenty-four hours to get out of town. Twenty-four. That's become my lucky number."

Fowler appeared immensely relieved. "No fooling?"

"No fooling. Do you know what Chet Anders is doing right now?

As a guess—kneeling by his bed. Praying that I'll get out of town and he won't be stuck with his brag.''

Fowler massaged his ear. ''Well, I've seen Chet in some terrible brannigans, Jim, and he's never lost yet. I mean, till today. So he might just be embarrassed enough to—''

Jim began to close the door. ''Go to bed, Joe. I'm going to spend tomorrow night between clean sheets, not in rock salt. I don't know about Chet, that's up to him.''

''He's a pretty rough boy, Jim. He was a guard in Santa Fe the time they had that scandal about the treatment of prisoners.''

''But I'm not a prisoner, Joe. So go to bed.''

Fowler, embarrassed, scratched his ear. ''Sure. Well, if you need anything—''

''Go to bed and stop worrying,'' Jim advised. He closed the door, snuffed out the lamp and lay on the hard leather springs. He did not worry about Anders. Tonight he worried about nothing. His happiness was deep and beautiful as a river. Tomorrow morning he would get right-of-way from Tom Sorrell and end the war with Hester. Old Mr. Dykes, who had engineered Travis' road, would appear in some ridiculous engineer's britches that engineers had not worn for twenty-five years and fuss around until Jim accepted him as adviser. Then he would start for Silver City with his rails. He would make enough money in a year to take it easy for three.

With a tingling he thought of Hester sleeping in the room next to him. She was a genuinely beautiful girl, with that red-tinged golden hair and those blue eyes. Reserved, but in time he would be able to guess what she was thinking. The trouble was, she thought too much. He wondered whether you made love to intelligent girls the same way you did to ordinary ones. He had made love to a girl quite a bit like Hester once, a girl he was too fond of, and he had spoiled it.

In the first five minutes with her she had let him kiss her, and afterward he was gloomy. Sitting close, she had pouted, ''You're disappointed in me, Jim,'' and he had said, ''Yep,'' and left her in her father's buggy. It wouldn't have mattered if he hadn't been in love with her.

Then he thought of Lovena. She came across his mind like a storm-shadow. His hand closed on the blanket. It had been thrilling to kiss her and tell her he loved her, but he had laid himself on a saw-edge because he had admitted to himself that he was in trouble. He had to finish this railroad, but what if he could not stay away from Lovena? He had to stay away from her. He was not in love with her. She was just very pretty and sweet, and he felt sorry for her, and the fact that she belonged to another man turned it into one of those situations where . . . In slow misery he struck the mattress with his fist.

Through the partition he heard Hester turn in bed. He wished he were in love with her. I could try to be, he thought. But that would be like trying to grow six inches. He lay there endeavoring to remember what he had been happy about a few minutes before.

In the morning the noise from the lobby woke him. A moody-eyed Mexican with dusty black hair brought shaving water. There was no sound from Hester Travis' room. After shaving, Jim brushed his coat and put it on. In the mirror above the marble-topped wash stand he looked fit, clean and business-like—gray-eyed, dark-haired, tanned. He would go out and impress people today and sell the ones who needed selling. He would make friends with them all. But the friendships he made would be current and useful, like newspapers, soon out-of-date.

With surprise he realized that since Drew Sullivan died he did not have one close friend. He made friends easily, yet he had none. He looked at the ruby on his finger. All his life his father had owned nothing finer than a cheap lodge ring and mail-order suit. And he, too, had few friends because he built friendships slowly, like houses.

Jim gave his lapels a tug to set the shoulders of his coat, polished his ruby on his sleeve, and went out.

The lobby was populated with ranchers and cattle buyers. As he walked through, Joe Fowler called to him from the desk. He signaled an old man who sat in a chair by the door. The old man got up and they met at the desk.

"Jim," Fowler said, "this is Clarence Dykes. Clarence, shake hands with Jim Harlan."

He was an odd looking man with the physique of a sand crane. He wore a black suit and a white shirt with a hard collar and no tie. His neck came up like a bundle of tendons. He had a very large nose, and when he gripped Jim's hand his fingers felt cold and hard as the foot of a bird. The thing which saved him from being laughable, Jim thought, was what he had in his head. He had laid out the smoothest ten miles of rails Jim had ever ridden over.

Mr. Dykes was abashed. "Sir, Divide is honored," he said. "Honored and grateful." It sounded like a little speech he had memorized.

"Pure business," Jim said easily. "But a pleasure too." He complimented Dykes on the tracks he had come over. It was the wrong thing to say before breakfast, because Dykes insisted that Jim come to his room and look at the plans he had drawn for the balance of the line.

"Well—well, sure," Jim said. You could not hurt this old man any more than you could slap a smiling child.

Dykes' room smelled of patent medicines and tobacco. It was littered with odd gear, and strung across the ceiling, like a coarse cobweb, was a system of cords which came to a focus beside the bed. Dykes tugged at one of them and the window grated up. He grinned at Jim's surprise.

"If you know anybody's got asthma, tell them this: Keep your room temperature constant. I can open the window, close the door, or adjust the damper of the stove without getting out of bed."

Jim said it was quite a contraption. But all it proved was that Dykes was odd, bored, and ingenious. Dykes found his plans in a commode and laid them out on the bed. Then he hesitated.

"Be honest with me. I don't want to force my ideas on anybody. But I've been working on plans ever since the Short Line folded. By heaven, a mule could pull a train up my grade now!"

Suddenly Jim's heart glowed, because he was going to do something for Clarence Dykes. Dykes knew those mountains and he had railroaded with General Dodge. "Mr. Dykes," he said, "will you work under me as assistant engineer? We'll use your plans all the way."

Dykes' eyes flooded. "That's pretty strong stuff," he said.

"I mean it. Between the two of us, we could build quite a railroad."

Dykes stood there with the proudest, most grateful expression a man had ever worn. "I'll work for nothing. I don't want a nickel.

Jim, Jim, do you know what it means to an old man to be recognized by a young one in his trade? Old men die of boredom! Con-ding-it, why do you think I've strung this room with a hundred yards of fish-line? And the problems of calculus and solid I've set myself! Anything to keep from losing my edge. I knew some day I'd be back at work. Ding it, Jim, railroad men have to build railroads, just like clocks have to tick!''

''They'll hear you ticking clear to Chicago after we finish this one. You're going to be rich on coal alone.''

''What's an old man need with money? All I ask is to be busy. Look here!''

He had to show Jim everything he had worked out. It took nearly an hour and Jim's stomach was growling. ''Get everything togeth-er,'' he said at last. ''I've got a little business to wind up and then in a few days we'll get out there and build us a railroad.''

Suddenly Dykes looked stricken. ''Tom Sorrell!'' he said. ''My lord, Jim, what'll you do about Tom Sorrell?''

Jim laughed. ''Everybody in town jumps when he says Tom Sorrell. I've got Sorrell in my pocket. I'm on my way to his ranch right now to get his right-of-way. I'll bet a pound of smoking tobacco to a can of Asthmador that I come back with his flower in my buttonhole.''

''You don't have to leave town to do it. He came in town last night. Keeps a room over the bank where he used to live most of the time before he married.''

Jim ate a breakfast steak at a cafe called Bill and Emma's, where a sauntering long-haired man with black Buffalo Bill mustaches served his coffee in a gilded mustache cup. Afterward he crossed the square to the bank. The street merged without boundary into the plaza, where wagons and buggies were parked and bull teams browsed in a teamster's corral. A fine Angus bull with a ring in his nose was tied to a post and a sign beside him advertised: *Ch. Dudley McOwen. Make date for service.* A cowman was talking to the owner, who sat brushing flies from the animal's eyes. Nearby, a Mexican cowboy was trying to train a balky horse to ride over a rope on the ground.

The bank stood by itself on the corner. A sheet-metal tunnel enclosed the outside stairway, with Sorrell's name on a card above the doorknob. It was unlocked and Jim went up. He could smell bacon and coffee. He knocked on the upper door and heard the dull ring of a man's spurs. With a cup of coffee in his left hand, Sorrell opened the door and looekd down at Jim on the step below. He wore black and gray pants tucked into yellow boots. In an undershirt with long sleeves, he had none of the big-rancher polish of yesterday morning. A cedar-handled Colt was holstered on his right thigh.

"Up early, for a financier," Sorrell said. Broad through the shoulders, heavy-boned, he had the look of easy power. Lather hid half his face and scraps of soap spotted the jaw he had shaved. In his eyes was the dull cynicism of a man who has rummaged all night through uneasy blankets without finding sleep.

"It's nine-thirty," Jim said. "I suppose that would seem early to a man of quality. Shall I come back later?"

Sorrell chuckled. "Get off it, Jim. Pour yourself some coffee."

He walked to a mirror hung above one end of a wooden drainboard. The room contained a cot, a stove for cooking and heating, and a galvanized-iron sink embedded in the wooden drainboard. Sorrell's shirt lay over the back of a chair and his coat hung from an antelope prong by the door. A short bronze-framed rifle leaned against the wall.

Jim sat down with his coffee. "Did Mrs. Sorrell tell you about the trouble with Hester Travis?"

Sorrell grunted as he flicked peppery lather into a basin. "It would be good if I could get your reports directly, instead of through my wife."

"Was I supposed to keep it secret from her? I ran into her at the fort and thought she'd see you before I did."

"What was she doing there?" Sorrell asked, frowning as he edged a sideburn.

"She said she was out for a ride."

"She told me she was doing a watercolor of the fort."

He turned then and gazed squarely into Jim's eyes. Jim's stomach rocked. "Maybe she did one after I left."

"Dick Spurlock said she left first."

"If Spurlock was there too, what's all the fuss? Look, I don't get this," Jim protested.

"Women are funny, Jim. Some of them like to flirt with a man and then slap him on the chops when he gets out of line. Maybe Lovena's like that. But just as a guess, it'll probably be me that slaps you on the chops instead of Lovena if you meet her alone again. *Claro?*''

"It was clear without your telling me. Now can we go ahead?"

"Let's do." Sorrell said. He bent to rinse the razor. "So you bungled things with Hester."

"She was looking for trouble before I ever got there. She's got the idea I'm sort of fast-shuffle man."

"You can't blame her for being smart." Sorrell chuckled.

A muscle hardened in Jim's jaw. "You don't seem worried about her taking me to court."

"That's because of my childlike trust in you. You told me yourself you were the smartest operator in railroading."

Jim grinned. "Hang onto that razor, now, Senator. I've already squared it with her. I've as good as got my right-of-way."

"The devil you say!" In the mirror, Sorrell actually looked disappointed.

"I talked her into a deal. If I could prove my ability by getting your signature, she'd let her uncle sign for her."

Sorrell emptied the basin, poured hot water and rinsed his face. He touched two small cuts on his chin with a stub of alum. "Take a seat up front, Jim. That's pretty good."

Jim settled down, his muscles stretching. He sipped the coffee and grimaced. Sorrell saw it and smiled.

"Too strong? That there's good old camp coffee, Jim. I'm a plain man. I eat plain and I talk plain. Now, see if this is plain enough for you to savvy—I'm not giving you any right-of-way until you show me Hester's!"

"Do I laugh now?" Jim snapped.

"If it seems funny. I kind of thought I'd hold back that paper as my hole card. We've got a lot of work ahead of us, and sometimes it seems to me we're not hitting the collars together. I figure that as long as you still need me, we'll be friends."

"Do you want this railroad built or not?"

"I want it started. Then I think we'd better slow down and look it all over good before we finish up. I don't think things are right for a railroad yet."

"Rawlings told me you made a pest of yourself, selling this railroad idea to Great Southern."

"Old Mart." Sorrell chuckled affectionately. "He's got his plans, I've got mine. He's sheared so many sheep in his day that I'm surprised he lay down under the clippers for me. The way I see this railroad going, you'll take it along for about fifteen miles and then run into trouble. Then you go bankrupt and I take over. That's why I think we ought to wait a while on my right-of-way."

Jim's eyes were steady and disrespectful. "I signed a paper with them."

"But my lawyer wrote it! You could strain rocks through the holes in it. You make any deal you want, Jim, hear? If you get a better offer from me, tell them to go to hell."

"They're paying my bills," Jim said doggedly.

"With cash, not checks. Because they don't want to be accused of doing anything the U. S. legal department wouldn't approve of. So they can't prove they paid them, can they?"

Jim studied him. Sorrell was pulling on his shirt. He was rough and solid and as unconcerned with morals as a timber wolf. "What do you want with a railroad?" Jim asked him. But suddenly he saw it. "Or is it a coal mine you want?"

"I just want money," Sorrell said. "Like you."

"What happens to Mr. Dykes?"

"Dykes will come out all right. What does a man his age need beside cocoa and dry toast?"

"Prestige," Jim said. *And the right to tick.* Dykes had said it with tears in his eyes. Dykes was probably pressing his engineer's pants right now, preparing for this grand windup as a railroad engineer. But it would be a windup in a dead-end canyon if Sorrell ever took charge. "All right," he said, "if you're going to sit on it we're both stopped. I can pack up and go home and you can forget any plans you had."

"How would you have handled it if she hadn't bought your idea of swapping my signature for hers?"

"I'd have bluffed. But Anders would make bluffing risky. He's got his ears back. He may come with a gun next time we tangle."

"You're not afraid of guns, are you?"

Jim was breathing shallowly. *I'm going to smash this fool,* he thought. "Is this what it takes to make a man rich?" he asked. "The mind and morals of an alley cat?"

Color darkened Sorrell's face. "Watch out, Jim. That pulpit's rocking under you."

"They want a railroad and I'm giving it to them."

"With triple rates after it's built. You're a real philanthropist, you are. You'll do business my way or not at all."

"You go to hell," Jim said.

Sorrell flipped his Colt from the holster. It was there silver-and-blue in his hand and he was walking forward staring into Jim's eyes. Jim shifted weight on one arm of the chair as he sat waiting. Sorrell pressed the muzzle of the revolver against his throat.

"Tough boy, Jim," he said. "But I figure there's at least one good crawl in you, and I'll bet I could find it if I went looking. What if I said, 'Jim, I figure you for a wife-stealer and a banty rooster trying to be an eagle and I'm going to kill you.' Would you bat an eye?"

Jim looked up at him. He heard the greased whisper of a spring in the Colt. He put his boot against the side of Sorrell's. He took his hand from the arm of the chair and showed his palm to Sorrell.

"Steady as stone," he said.

Sorrell looked at Jim's open hand. Jim slapped his other hand up and caught the gun barrel. He whipped his fist into the side of Sorrell's head, and caught Sorrell's foot as he sprawled away. Sorrell landed on his side. But he rolled over so fast that Jim did not have time to tap him with the Colt. Jim lunged up out of the chair just as Tom Sorrell reached the carbine beside the door. Sorrell turned in the posture of kneeling rifleman, on one knee and one foot, and Jim saw his face totally without varnish, with all his rage and strength gouged into it. He saw his hand take the loading lever down.

CHAPTER 11

JIM COULD SEE into the open breech of the gun where a blunt copper shell gleamed. The hammer of the carbine was back and when Tom Sorrell slapped the lever home he would be ready to fire.

"Hold it," Jim said. "If you close it I'll shoot."

Sorrell's hand started the upswing. Jim's arm tightened for the kick of the revolver. He saw the white spot on the rancher's cheekbone where his fist had hit him. He aimed at Sorrell's right shoulder; the rifle covered the left. They faced each other across the bare floor. Then Sorrell slowly lowered the gun and reached to lean it against the wall. He breathed like a hurt stallion. Jim uncocked the Colt and threw it on the bed. He felt drained.

"This is a hell of a start," he said. "What's the matter with you? Isn't life tough enough?"

With his mouth set, Tom Sorrell stood up. In pants and unbuttoned shirt, his dark hair mussed, he did not look like the wealthy rancher and cowtown politician he was, nor did this room which he called his camp seem in character. But they were all a part of Sorrell.

Sorrell said, "Life's tough enough without having your wife lie to you, or having a Fancy Dan try to tell you how it's going to be. Get it straight, Harlan—you're not going anywhere without me."

"Nor with you, the way your're going. Was that a bluff or did you mean to do it?"

Sorrell started buttoning his shirt. "I can get mad enough to kill, but I wouldn't study on it first. That was to show you I meant business. You can get out of here when you're ready."

"Do you want a railroad built or not?" Jim was trying to cool his anger and be reasonable.

Sorrell took his coat from the chair where it had lain. Holding it in both hands, he stared at Jim. The bruise on his cheek was red, now. "Try to savvy this," he said. "There's going to be a railroad built and it's going to be built my way. You can walk just so far across a canyon on faith. Then you fall in. I figure you're not far enough across to make the far side, but you're too far to go back."

Jim went to the door. He turned quickly to stare at Sorrell. "Do I get your right-of-way after I get Hester's?"

Sorrell smiled as he pulled on the coat. "Let's talk about that at the proper time."

Jim went out and slammed the door. He heard the rifle slide down and clatter on the floor. He descended the hot, dusty tunnel of the stairs. He could feel the heat piercing the sheet metal. The street was warm and dusty, and down the way the stage from El Paso was taking on passengers while a man in shirtsleeves stood on the walk looking at his watch. A run of red-necked cattle were being corraled in the plaze. Jim stood in the shade, tossing a coin on his hand. He could see a clock before a shop next to the hotel. Eleven-twenty. He was supposed to have met Hester at eleven.

She would tell him, with that wise little smile, *All right, then, Mr. Harlan, you can move your car off my land by tonight.*

He felt as if his mind were wading through deep mud. He was running a race without a finish and without a start. If she says *Anders* to me, he thought, I'll . . . And again it was a thing he could not finish.

Well, he thought, let's snap out of it.

He settled his Stetson, pushed back the tails of his coat to slip his hands in his pockets, and left the walk.

Joe Fowler's lobby rocked with the voices and cigar smoke of its out-of-towners and local ranchers. Jim looked around without seeing Hester, but from the desk Flower beckoned him. As Jim approached, Fowler moistened the tips of his fingers and slicked down the reddish hair above his ears, bashful and hearty.

"Miss Hester found the lobby a little—well, let's be frank—a little rough. She asked you to wait when you came in and she'd be right out."

"I'll be right here." Jim put his elbow on the counter.

He cleaned his nails with a golden pen-knife. In a moment Hester came toward him, a tall, slender girl who held her skirts from the floor with one hand. She was smiling and Jim quickly removed his hat and assumed a smile. But when he did so, Hester ceased smiling. He had not carried it off. He could not fool her one bit. Fowler went into his wicketed preserve and Jim heard him humming as he sorted mail. He was a booster. Boosters loved progress and Joe Fowler thought progress was taking place in his hotel.

This morning, Hester's face was exceptionally pretty, color glowing along her cheekbones like wildflowers and her eyes as bright as gem-stones.

"Miss Hester," Jim said, holding her hand, "you told me you used rouge sometimes, but I never thought it would be in the daytime. I swear no girl has so much natural color."

Smiling sadly, Hester shook her head. "It's no good, Mr. Harlan. A good try, but no good."

"Well, it's early," Jim conceded. "Shall we walk under the *portales?*" He took her arm, but Hester freed it gently.

"About Tom Sorrell," she said.

"Always the businesswoman," Jim sighed. "The business with Sorrell is—indefinite. Not signed, not refused. He won't be pressed."

Hester tucked a wisp of hair in place. Through her severity he saw a shadow of disappointment. "I'm sorry," she said. "I'm very sorry. Will you tell me one thing? What *is* definite about your railroad?"

"Two things. Your opposition to it, and your uncle's approval. By any chance have you seen him this morning?"

"No, and I'm a little concerned. Ordinarily he rolls up in a horse blanket somewhere along the trail and reaches town early. Well—" She sighed and rubbed her palms together. "I have a twelve o'clock appointment with Francis McKenna, my lawyer. I'd hoped to break it."

Jim gripped her hands. "If I could just have a week!"

"If you had a week," Hester said drily, "you'd get up a head of steam no one could release without blowing up the whole town. Stock, indeed! And probably personal loans on the side. Last night I thought I might have been wrong about you. This morning I'm sure I was right. You told me you had Tom Sorrell in your pocket. Well, which pocket was it—in your other coat?''

"Sorrell's no fool. He wants time to write a letter. I suppose he means to check on my facts and be sure I can expose him.''

"Why don't you pressure him, as you're trying to pressure me? And will you please let go of my hand?''

Joe Fowler had stopped humming. He was staring at them. He came from the pigeon holes. "Miss Hester, if you don't mind a well-meant word of advice—''

Moisture shone in Hester's eyes. "I do, though, Joe. Yesterday I accused Mr. Harlan of being a confidence man. Today I make the same accusation. I gave him an opportunity to prove himself. He failed. I'm going ahead now with my plan to do all I can to stop him.''

A man near the desk said, "Harlan?''

Jim glanced around, frowning. It was Sorrell's foreman, Dick Spurlock. "Hello,'' he said. Spurlock's cocky, assured grace annoyed him. He had come in with his Comanche skill at blending into a background. He stood there in a pony-skin vest and town pants and a dove-gray Stetson with a beaded band. Spurlock removed his hat and made Hester a little bow.

"Sorry to carry bad news,'' he said.

"Bad news!''

Spurlock smiled. "For Mr. Harlan. I don't know, maybe it's a joke. Chet Anders says he wants to see you, Harlan.''

Hester opened her lips to speak, but closed them and gazed at Jim. Then she said, "If you'll take my advice, you won't go.''

"Do you think I'm afraid of your wild bull?'' Jim retorted. "Where is he?'' Spurlock curled the brim of his hat, watching Jim.

Jim made Hester a bow that was a mockery of Spurlock's and a travesty of politeness. "With your permission,'' he said.

Hester glanced at Dick Spurlock. "Does he—is he carrying—''

"Who isn't? Roundup time everybody carries a side-arm.''

Jim gazed candidly into Hester's face. "I hope you like the show. You've gone to a lot of trouble to arrange it. I hear there's going to be a cock fight in the plaza, if this doesn't satisfy your taste for excitement.''

Spurlock caught his arm as he thrust into the traffic of the boardwalk. Jim glanced at him. Spurlock's Stetson rested on the side of his head and his neat, freckled features were sharp. Spurlock told him, "Here—let's get off the walk." They stepped from the arcaded coolness into the street. A traffic of buggies, drays, farm wagons and horses resounded about them. The tall foreman moved close to Jim. He flicked a speck of dust from the shoulder of Jim's jacket.

"I should think a man in your spot would be damned careful," he said. "I saw you with the boss' wife yesterday."

"And you couldn't wait to get to the boss," Jim suggested.

"Give me credit for better sense. The boss would kill you both, and me for telling him. Harlan, you must be crazy to take a chance like that."

"Ever been in love?" Jim asked him.

Spurlock's hazel eyes looked withdrawn with dislike. "Yes, but I've never been crazy."

"Then you weren't in love. Is that what you wanted to tell me— how to conduct myself?"

Spurlock moved back a foot. "I can keep quiet. Some men can't. And no woman could, if she knew what was going on. *Is* there anything going on?"

Jim smiled. "Ask her. Or are you too cagey for that—afraid you'd tip your own hand? There's no use being cagey with your mouth if you're going to trail her all over the range."

Spurlock stepped back to the walk, stiff and hot-eyed. Then Jim heard the whisper of something falling. He glanced up, but the sun's sharpness blinded him. He felt something touch his Stetson and drop on down, brushing his arm and falling to the ground. Above him, on the upper gallery of the hotel, he saw someone leaning across the railing and holding a rope in the manner of a man raising a bucket of water from the well. He recognized the face of Chet Anders.

Jim knew what was happening, then. He darted for the walls, but the noose picked up his feet and he sprawled hard at full length. His hat rolled away. The wind was knocked out of him. A buggy whirled by and he felt the jar of wheels near his head. He started to scramble up, hearing Anders' shout of laughter, but Anders spilled him again and began to haul up on the rope. Jim clutched at the ground. He spun into the air with his hands full of earth. A man on the boardwalk shouted, "Look here, boys!" Then at once a dozen of them were laughing. Jim could see their faces as they ran into the street to watch. Dick Spurlock, leaning against a post, was lighting a cigarette.

Jim began to flop like a fish, trying to catch the rope which cinched his ankles, but Anders kept joggling the rope. Jim's money and keys jingled on to the ground. His coat skirts fell down over his face. Anders was moving along the rail.

Jim made himself let go. Reaching up, he loosened his string tie and collar. The ground was not far below him. He heard Hester's voice.

"Chet, for mercy sake what are you doing?"

"I'm workin' on a theory, Miss Hester. What goes up must come down, Right? Now, see here."

He made a bight of the rope about the gallery rail so that he had both hands free. Jim saw him look up at the stubby flagpole which extended out over the street from the timbering above his head. The foreman tossed the free end of the rope over the pole and caught it. Then he flipped the bight loose and supported Jim's weight pulley-wise.

"Now, then, I've got this rope bent across the flagpole, right? If I'm to get down and he's to come up, it'll have to do for a pulley. All right, watch!"

Jim had a queer foreshortened view of the foreman. While he watched, Anders swung himself over the railing and sat there an instant. The men in the street became silent. Wagons and buggies were halting. Jim's heart squeezed tight. Anders looked down, grinning. Then, clutching the rope tightly, he jumped out over the street.

Jim shot up with a yank. Spurs raked his chest as Anders dropped past, and then Anders was on the ground and men were laughing. Bill Holly, the Muleshoe range boss, had run up. He struck Anders on the back and said something to Hester. Jim's feet were nearly touching the flagpole. He dangled just out of reach of the porch railing. Chet Anders tied the rope to a hitch-rack. Then he walked to his horse and snatched a pigging string from the saddle. He soaked it in the horse trough and tossed it to Bill Holly.

"Hike up there and tie his feet," he said.

Holly glanced quizzically at Hester. "It's all right," she said.

Jim began to thresh again, but he could not reach and hold the rope long enough to free his feet. He fell back, panting.

A black cross-bar buggy with red wheels flashed into view with a young woman driving it. It was Lovena. She drew her horses to a halt and stared up at Jim. He tried to grin at her. Bill Holly emerged on the upper gallery.

He managed to reach and tie Jim's ankles snugly with the wet rope. Jim heard him chuckle, "Yes, sir, this is sure a tough old Texan! Tougher'n butter in a hot pipe!"

Jim reached in his pocket for his knife. Then he saw it below him—a slim golden finger in the dust.

Jim had a curious view of the road and the plaza. He twisted slowly so that the street appeared to revolve. Colors were intensified. He recalled a theory that sunsets looked more beautiful if you viewed them standing on your head. He was fairly sure it would not be worthwhile.

Next, he saw Lovena descend from the buggy with the whip in her hand. She came up behind Chet Anders, raised it and struck angrily at the foreman's broad back. Then someone caught the lash and yanked it from her, and the next time Jim's turnings brought her in view, he saw that it was Hester. The street was silent. The sounds were all distant ones. The girls confronted each other, the tall, slender blonde and the brunette with the finest figure you could imagine. Suddenly Lovena leaned over to pick up Jim's knife. She opened it and marched smartly past Hester. She reached the rack where the rope was tied. Then Hester caught her shoulders and turned her.

"Will you please leave things as they are, Mrs. Sorrell?" she cried.

"Yes—as they were before your insane foreman came along!" Lovena retorted.

She turned to the rope again and she started to cut. Jim shouted but she did not seem to hear. Once more Hester intervened. She tore the knife from Lovena and threw it down. There was blood on her hand and she put it to her mouth. She put a handkerchief over the cut and faced Lovena.

"Do you want to kill the man? Don't you know if you cut the rope he'll fall on his head?"

Jim was growing so dizzy that the street had begun to bulge like an over-inflated pig's bladder. Everything had a shimmering mother-of-pearl quality. He saw Lovena glance up and catch both hands to her breast. He heard her call to him.

"Jim, what do you want me to do?"

"Get—get—" He could not think of whom to tell her to get. If he had a friend in this town . . .

Suddenly old Dykes came from the hotel. All Jim saw was his black suit and stonelike bald head as he strode to the hitch-rack. Dykes began to untie the rope. He thrust Hester away when she tried to stop him. There was a steady roar of underground water in Jim's ears. He saw Chet Anders move up and swing Dykes around with one hand and smash a fist into his jaw. Dykes staggered back against a porch support and sat down. His long chin came to rest against his chest. A burlap-colored dog came along to sniff at him.

Anders' voice seemed to ascend from the bottom of a well. "Swear to Johnny I don't know what to do about him myself, boys! I reckon I'll mosey down to the Gold Exchange and have a drink on it. Anybody else? And he better be just like that when I come back, else I'll peel the hide right off the man who lets him down."

Anders mounted and pulled from the rack. A few men went with him. Jim tried again to reach his ankles, succeeded and put desperate fingers to the hard, wet rope. The knot had set like concrete. He fell back. The moorings of the flagpole gave forth wooden protests. Blood seemed to soak into Jim's brain like a sponge. He remembered that Travis was due in town this morning. Travis would help him. He tried to see that hope clearly, like a bead he was trying to pluck from a stream.

CHAPTER 12

TOM SORRELL watched it from the plaza. He was there to see his wife come in town and witness her struggle with Hester Travis over helping Jim Harlan. Sorrell's temper smoldered like green wood. He had told Lovena to stay at the ranch. She had disobeyed. When on top of that he found her engaged in a hair-pulling match over Harlan, it rubbed him like emery. After Chet Anders went down the street he saw Lovena turn to the men who still stood there.

"Is everyone afraid of that bully except a woman and an old man?" No one replied. The crowd began to crumble away.

Sorrell stood in the dust with the muscles rigid in his jaw. So in an hour everyone in Divide would know that the wife of Tom Sorrell had fought with Hester Travis over Jim Harlan. By damn, a horse-whipping might be what she needed! His impulse was to take her to his room over the bank. He would have some words with Dick Spurlock, too. He had not given him permission to come in town today. Lovena had probably brought him along as an escort.

But against his urge to punish Lovena he set the need to talk to Anders. The foreman was a cool one—a murderer last night; as arrogant as ever this morning. He saw Anders jogging away on his pony and made his choice. He crossed the plaza and reached the Gold Exchange just as Anders finished tying his pony. Anders pulled his carbine from the scabbard and ducked under the rack. Then he saw Tom Sorrell waiting beside the door. Sorrell gazed at him curiously. To his amusement, Anders was still acting the town-boss.

"What the hell do *you* see, mister?" the foreman snapped.

"The same old face, Chet, only I hardly recognized it. Horse kick you?"

Anders snorted. "Yes, and I just hung him up for skinning." He juggled the rifle in his hand, gave Sorrell a stare and butted the slatted door open with his shoulder. Sorrell sauntered after him.

Inside the saloon it was dark and cool as a winter afternoon. Sorrell placed himself on the angle of the bar so he could watch Anders, who had stopped, facing the backbar, and thumped his rifle down on the varnish. Pearlie Owen, the saloonkeeper, came along the bar. There was a good pre-lunch crowd to keep Pearlie's three bartenders busy. They came and went through sawdust which smelled like pencil sharpenings.

"Something?" Pearlie asked Anders. Pearlie was a bullet-headed, stiff-necked little man whose apron fell from his armpits like a tube.

Tom Sorrell tapped a coin on the counter. "Whiskey for the cowboy and myself, Pearlie."

Anders gazed woodenly at him. "Don't spoil me, Mr. Sorrell." He tossed out his own coin.

Men were looking at them. Sorrell said agreeably, "That Muleshoe pay must be getting better, Chet." Just then he noticed Anders' new ducking-cloth jacket.

"I ain't working for Muleshoe," Anders said.

"What happened?"

"Travis's got his ideas, I got mine," Anders said. "Did he come in town yet?" he asked Bill Holly.

"Ain't seen him. He went up to Jacinto's after he left the siding yesterday."

"You reckon he's dodging me? He owes me some money."

Holly smiled. "He's good for it, Chet. He had seven thousand cattle the last time we counted them."

Sorrell watched Anders' smile to himself as he rubbed the walnut butt of his gun. "That was rotten timing, Chet," Sorrell said.

Everyone looked at Sorrell except Anders. A little whiskey slopped from the foreman's glass. "I don't get you."

"You quitting Travis when you did."

Anders' hazel eyes turned. "Why?"

"You should have stuck it another twenty-four hours. You might have been boss man over there."

Anders could not take his gaze from Sorrell's face. "Why would I?" he asked without inflection.

"Because Travis is dead," Sorrell said.

Out among the tables a man said enthusiastically to another," . . . and danged if them critters didn't throw true every time!" and there was a sound of a cork popping. Pearlie Owen dropped a bottle opener. Two men backed from the bar to stare at Sorrell. Except for a few out-of-towners, every man at the bar turned to look at the rancher.

"He always would ride a green-broke bronc," Sorrell said. "I found him in Lopez Canyon last night. He'd gone over the bank. His neck was broken." He told them about it. He did not pull on any sactimonious gloom. They all knew of his enmity with Travis. "I sent Jacinto for help. I thought the wagons would be in by now. But I suppose they're traveling slow."

Bill Holly rubbed his jaw, staring at Anders. Suddenly he said, "I'm going to meet them!" Several men went with him. Others began questioning Sorrell. He talked, had another whiskey, and continued to watch Anders, who had not spoken. The room was loud with conversation now, and the patrons were splitting into small vociferous groups.

"So I reckon you're looking for work," Sorrell said to Anders.

"One job's about the same as another," Anders said. "Maybe so Mrs. Travis will want me to stay on. That's a damn' shame," he pronounced.

Sorrell said philosophically, "Well, so it goes," and left the bar. As he passed Anders, he touched the foreman's new jacket. "Tough," he said. "Ought to last. Takes toughness to last anywhere, eh?"

He went outside. Harlan was still hanging heels-up before the hotel. Anders slammed from the saloon and stared up and down the walk. Then he turned his head and saw Sorrell beside the door. He came belligerently toward him.

"What'd that mean, mister?"

"What'd what mean?"

"About my jacket."

"You're smart, Chet. You figure it out."

Anders gripped Sorrell's arm. "Don't be cute with me, mister. You got anything to say, say it!"

Sorrell said, "All right, Chet, I'll say it. I mean I can send you to the gallows. I saw you kill Cam Travis."

"You're dreaming," Anders scoffed. A scar showed on his cheek as his color faded.

"No, I'm not," Sorrell said. "I wrote it down just the way I saw it and mailed myself a registered copy of the statement. They'll hold it in the post-office until I call for it. I put another copy in the safe at the bank."

"How many whiskies did you have in there?" Anders asked. "If you did see anything like that, you'd go to the sheriff, not write it down and mail it around."

"How do you know what I'd do?"

Anders glanced at Sorrell and quickly looked away again. He put his back to the broken plaster front of the saloon. Sorrell could see his mind slowly putting the pieces together—where he had slipped; whether Sorrell could ever come back at him if he didn't tell on him now. Tom Sorrell had had most of the night to think about it and he had his arguments ready.

"I'm going out today and look for your jacket," he told Anders. "If you burned it, that would be as bad as throwing it in the brush. Copper buttons don't burn, but they might hang a man. Whatever I find I'll save it. If I have to, I'll produce it and say I thought it was you I saw kill Travis, but I didn't want to say until I had the proof."

Anders' stony gaze roved the plaza. Sorrell chuckled and laid a hand on his shoulder. "Where's the bull of the town, now?" he asked. "Why don't you tell me not to get cute?"

"What are you getting at?" Anders asked. His hand pulled a bit of broken plaster from the wall behind him.

"I'm not getting at anything, except that friends should hang together. Maybe some day I'll need you to do something for me."

"Oh, ho!" Anders said, without recapturing his bravado.

"Oh, ho," Sorrell repeated. "And when I do, you'll know what I'm talking about. You can do one thing for me today—buy yourself a tablet and write me a letter. Just say that you slugged Cam Travis and crowded his horse off the trail. Then you cut the horse's throat so it wouldn't suffer and got rid of the jacket you were wearing because it was covered with blood. Take it to the post-office and drop it. They'll put it in my box. If it isn't there by sundown, I'll turn you in.''

He moved from the wall, settled his Stetson and nodded at Anders. ''Yes, sir, that sure is a nice jacket. Tough. I hope you're worthy of it, Chet. If you are, you'll always have a job with me, whatever happens around Muleshoe.''

And he gave Anders a grin. It was meant to imply: I'm no preacher myself; I like a man with guts; you can trust me. It must have got across, because Chet Anders grinned back and winked.

Sorrell had not forgotten Lovena. The triumph he felt over Chet's coming to heel became part of an angry sheen of power. So he could handle a man like Anders, but his own wife was as hard-mouthed as a bronc! Sorrell strode purposefully to the hotel. Harlan was still swinging head down from Anders' rope, but Clarence Dykes and Day Clevis were lowering him, now. Sorrell glanced about for Lovena in the small crowd, but could not find her. A gusty anger swept him. By heaven, if she had come to town to hide from him and take up her troubles with Harlan . . . !

He stepped into the street to search the plaza. Wait, he thought. She's gone to my room. He moved across the bustling square. The tin-roofed stairway was hot enough to ignite paper. Sorrell flung open the door and gazed about the room but saw only his own dirty dishes and rumpled cot. He felt the sharp teeth of panic. No, he decided, she's gone to the bank to get money for train fare. He hurried back down the stairs. She was not in the bank, but the manager said she had been in earlier.

''How much did she draw out?'' Sorrell asked.

''Four hundred dollars,'' the manager said. ''She said you'd need it this morning.''

''That's right, Charlie,'' Sorrell said. ''I wanted to be sure it was ready. Thanks. Lots of business?''

''Never better.''

Sorrell's eyes were like stone when he came from the bank. He gazed across the plaza at the trees and low structures of the town. Never had he thought of it as being a warren of rooms, but this was how he saw it now. A thousand rooms and Lovena was in one of them. She would not have dared leave by daylight. Then his mind focused down on a single room in the Home Ranch Hotel, and his hand clenched on the coins in his pocket.

He walked quickly across the plaza to the hotel where Harlan was staying.

CHAPTER 13

AFTER THEY helped him into his room, Jim lay for a long time on the bed. His brain gave a sick squeeze every time he tried to sit up. He lay there listening to Day Clevis and Clarence Dykes talk about Cam Travis.

"I can't believe it," Clevis said in his slow fashion. "Cam Travis was the heart of this basin. It'll die too."

"That's no way to talk," Dykes said. "There's Divine reasoning in it. The day he died, Jim Harlan came. The railroad will do for us what Cam Travis always tried to. Cam died knowing that."

Jim closed his eyes. Suddenly he came up on one elbow. "Say! What was that about Cam Travis?"

Dykes told him. Travis had been brought in by Jacinto Chavez and some cowboys. Jim sank back. "If I thought my railroad had anything to do with this—"

"Hogwash!" Dykes said. "It's true the horse was green broke. Cam shouldn't have rode it at night." Then he gave a little laugh, but there were tears in his eyes. "Talk about foresight. When we took him to Paul Fleming's, Paul told me he'd had his headstone in his back room for ten years. Cam had him order it and save it. Paul let me see what Cam said about himself—'The best cowman and the worst poet in New Mexico.' "

"It's too bad for Mrs. Travis," Jim said numbly.

"It is, it is," Day Clevis said. "We're going right out to see her. I expect," he said uneasily, "that Hester will run the place now."

There was a knock on the door and Dykes went to open it. He was wearing some curious tight-legged breeches in which he had, without question, worked in the Union Pacific. Dykes grunted in displeasure after he opened the door. "We're busy," he said.

Jim heard Tom Sorrell's voice. The rancher came into the doorway and Jim looked at him. "How's the daring young man?" Sorrell asked.

"Right end up again," Jim said.

There were brusque lines at the corners of Sorrell's mouth. He seemed to search for something, his eyes rummaging the room. Dykes asked him what he wanted. "Just asking after our handsome young friend," the rancher said. "I was a little worried that his brains might have been addled. Since he seems to be in good condition, I'll say *adios.*"

"*Adios,*" Jim said. Sorrell closed the door.

"You know each other?" Day Clevis asked. His Mexican-black eyes were curious.

"Since this morning. I hit him up for a right-of-way. He's bucking a little, but he'll come around. Do you know if Hester's left town?" he asked.

"Don't reckon she has," Dykes replied. "The little hussy! Setting Anders to torment a man like that! Why, if that rope had broke—"

"Will you get her for me? And fetch that writing paper. Write this down—" He waited until Dykes was sitting with the tablet on his knees. "Telegram to A. J. Purdy, Cincinnati, Ohio. He's my Eastern agent," he explained. " 'Send first group workmen and twelve flats basic supplies.' " Purdy was the code name for Mark Rawlings of Great Southern.

Dykes wrote it. He had an approving grin for Jim. "That's telling her, Jim. You get some certificates printed up, because there's already a dozen men asking to buy."

"In good time," Jim said uneasily. "Send her in as you go out, eh? Her room's next to mine. I'd kind of like to talk to her alone."

Dykes gave him the draft of the telegram. Day Clevis set his broad-brimmed hat on the side of his head to cover his gotched ear, told Jim to take it easy, and went out with Dykes. In a moment Hester came to the door. She gazed at Jim but did not enter.

"I'm glad you're better," she said. "But now you know I wasn't fooling."

Jim picked up the tablet. Rumpled and frowning, he sat on the edge of the bed. "Here's a copy of a telegram I'm sending my agent in the East," he said.

Hester merely raised her shoulders as he read. "It'll only be that much more grief for you," she said. "Now, I want you to understand exactly how I feel about you. I not only blame you for making my uncle's last thoughts of me bitter ones, but for his death."

"Oh, now, wait!"

"Because if he hadn't been hurrying to meet you, he wouldn't have ridden at night on a steep trail."

Jim shook his head. "Women!" he said. "Was he so poor a rider? Wasn't he on the county road?"

"The fact remains—oh, why discuss it? The fact is, you aren't going to build a railroad without an army to clear the way for you. Is that quite clear?"

A man cleared his throat. Hester glanced over her shoulder at the hall and saw the Mexican porter who had brought Jim's shaving water that morning. "I hope thou goest well?"

"I go fine," Jim said. He saw the envelope the man carried. "Mail for me?"

"*Si.*"

Hester took the letter and Jim reached for it, but she glanced at the inscription. Then with a half-implied smile she handed it to him. The inscription was as feminine as sachet. Jim tossed it face down on the bed.

"Is Mrs. Sorrell going to help with your stock sales?" Hester asked.

Jim put his hand on the letter. "That's not from Mrs. Sorrell."

"I thought I knew the green ink." Hester smiled.

"No, it's from a lady who monograms my handkerchiefs." He stretched out on the bed again. "I'm supposed to rest."

He could hear her breathing. She seemed trying to phrase something important. "Aren't you curious about your mail?"

"No, but I can see you are."

"I can't help wondering why Mrs. Sorrell should be writing you. Did you know her before you came to Divide?"

Sighing, Jim sat up and opened the letter. "It's from my sister.

She says the baby's had summer complaint. And they had a light
frost but it didn't kill the alfalfa. Can I rest now?''

"Frost never kills alfalfa."

"That's right. Her writing's hard to follow."

As he lay down, he heard her petticoats rustle. The door creaked.
"Don't forget," she reminded, "what I said about moving your
car."

"No. If you decide to wreck it, remember what I said I'd do."

"Cut off my hair?" She laughed. "I'd like to see you try!"

The door closed. Jim sat up quickly. Dusk was gathering in the
room and he carried the letter to the window.

> *"Jim, dear. I'll be at my milliner, Mrs. Bailey's, when you
> get this. You must help me get to La Cinta. I've left Tom, shall
> explain when I see you. I shall never go back. If you will meet
> me at Fort Quanah tonight, we can be in La Cinta by morning
> and I can be on the train. Shall leave Divide after dark. Do
> help me!"*

Do help me! Do help me what? Get us both shot? Jim made scraps
of the letter, gave it to the wind in the slot of alley outside the
window and pulled out his watch. Four o'clock. What in heaven did
she want to do? Ride double to La Cinta? Drive a buggy on the
country road with her husband after them? In a way he was glad that
she had come to him for help. She could have asked Spurlock. But
he felt she had shotgunned him into something with sure catastrophe
at the end of it.

Yet there was no question of his failing her. He lay down to wait
for dark.

Later he ate at Bill and Emma's crowded counter where for the
second time, the langorous counterman with a towel tucked under
his belt brought coffee in a mustache cup.

Afterward he took his horse from the hotel stable and left town by
a back road. There was a snap in the air, a promise of early frost. He
cut over to the county road after he had cleared all the outlying
farms. On the open road he felt like a buck in cougar country. Under
a low moon the road ran like a pale tape through the hills. Now he

knew why Sorrell had come to his room. He was looking for
Lovena. He would still be looking for Lovena, and after finishing in
Divide he probably would set out on the county road. Jim ground his
teeth and glanced back.

He came to a brush thicket beside the road where a fire blazed.
Some freighters had penned their oxen in a rope corral and were
making their shakedown here. Jim skirted their camp. He crossed a
wooden bridge over a wash, and suddenly a voice came up at him
out of the dark *barranca*. His horse reared.

"Jim! It's you, isn't it?"

"Great snakes!" Jim said, "give a man some warning!" He left
his pony by the road and slid down the bank. She was waiting for
him beside her horse, a hooded cape thrown back from her head and
her arms reaching to him. As he caught her, Jim felt her trembling.
She pressed against him.

"Thank heaven! Jim, I've been dying of fright."

"Well, I wasn't getting much reading in, either. Did it have to be
like this? Couldn't you have got word to me so I could get things
fixed up?"

"Jim, you're not scolding me for coming to you?"

"No, but I'm worried. What if Tom saw me leave? Or Spurlock?
He should wear mocassins and braid his hair. He's more Injun than
he is white."

"I had to come today, Jim. I couldn't stay with Tom another
hour."

"Couldn't you have stayed with some woman friend for a few
days? The first place he'll look for you will be where I am."

"Jim, dear, are you afraid of him too? Everyone is afraid of him.
But I thought you wouldn't be."

"I'm afraid that if he finds us together there'll be shooting." He
pulled her pony around and Lovena watched him.

"You make it sound so perilous! I thought—well, I had Dick
Spurlock take my bags to your car. I thought you could take me up to
the main line and get me on a train there."

Jim turned his head. "How could you trust that Apache?"

"He's fond of me. He wouldn't do anything to put me in
danger."

But Jim remembered that Spurlock had helped Anders hang him

by the heels this afternoon. Spurlock loved Lovena and hated Jim because she had come to him for help. "He isn't fond of me," Jim said. "I only hope he doesn't hate me enough to betray you to your husband."

She was very still. "You're trying to frighten me."

Jim held her by the shoulders. "I don't want you to be frightened. But I want you to know what could happen."

Her mouth trembled. "You want me to go back to him, don't you? Well, I can't! I'll never go back. I've never thrown myself at a man this way before, and I'm sorry I had to. If you want me to go on alone, I'll do it." Her eyes were big and full of tears.

Jim smiled and kissed her lips. They were cold. He could feel the fear in her. "If you'd thrown yourself at anyone else I'd have gone to work forgetting you. In fact I think I will anyway. But I'll get you out of here first."

She let him help her onto the side saddle. She was relaxing now. "You'd better not forget me. Because when you come to Cincinnati you'll find me forgetting you with a beau on each arm."

"I'll find that anyway. You're a born flirt. I'll just be the one who helped you get away." He had begun to believe it, but she laughed, taking it as banter. They put the horses up the bank to the road.

They let the horses trot. Night-hawks swooped across the road. A cold wind combed the brush. Suddenly Jim thought he heard a horse behind them. He twisted to stare down the winding aisle through the brush. Then he turned back, not yet certain what he had heard. Lovena talked, relieved and excited, like a girl who had nearly missed a train and now sat back in her chair, turning it all over to someone else. But Jim was silent, thinking that love was such a big thing to happen to you, it ought to be right. It went into your heart as smoothly as a fishhook, but it tore you coming out. A love that started like this—could it ever be right? Or were you always on a dark road looking over your shoulder, in the end not trusting even one another.

All at once he knew there was a horse behind them. Above the scuffing of their own mounts he heard the hard ring of a shod hoof.

"Did you tell Spurlock when you were going to leave?" he asked Lovena.

"Yes. Wasn't it all right?"

"Then maybe it's just him following us."

She stared back. "Oh, Jim! If it isn't—"

Jim thumped the saddlehorn with his knuckles, studying the road for landmarks. "I think the fort's pretty close." he told her. "Ride ahead and wait for me there. If you hear a horse coming, take off. If it's me, I'll whistle from the road."

She clutched his arm. "But if it's Tom—what will you tell him?"

"That I'm heading back to camp. Go along. I'll handle him." He struck her pony with his hat. He tried to smile at her, but he didn't have a smile left in him. After she rode on he cocked his revolver but left it in the holster. The horse was coming on at a high trot. Spurlock or Sorrell, or merely a cowboy in a hurry? he wondered. He pulled to the side of the road to wait.

He heard the horse snorting as it came along the wide lane through the brush, and knew it had been ridden long and hard. Its bridle chains jingled. Jim made out the dark horse-and-rider silhouette. He waited at the edge of the road. The rider saw him and lifted the head of the horse sharply as he set the bit back in its mouth. They stared at each other, and Jim recognized the square-shouldered form before he made out the features of Tom Sorrell.

"Just the nice time of day to ride, eh?" he said.

"What are you doing?" Sorrell demanded. "Had your belly full of Magdalena Basin?"

"Not quite. I'm going back to my camp."

"Always ride this late?"

"Only when I have to."

"Why did you have to tonight?"

"Just felt like riding," Jim said.

Sorrell's horse moved up, tossing its head. "Don't smart-talk me, Harlan!" the rancher said. "Where's Lovena?"

"Mrs. Sorrell," Jim said, "is one worry I haven't taken on yet."

Sorrell gave him a long, bridling glare. Then he dismounted to examine the tracks on the road by match-light. But the pocket dust had been trampled by scores of stage horses, ponies, and oxen. He straightened and let the match die in the dust.

"You'd better ride along to the fort with me. That'd make as good a rendezvous as any."

"I'll ride with you," Jim said. "But only because I'm going that way."

Sorrell's features were dogged with stifled fury. "Then that saves me making you do something you don't want to." He swung up and they moved out.

In about fifteen minutes Jim caught a silver-black flash of water on the flats below and to their right, and knew they were approaching the fort. The moon was up and soon the dead, roofless buildings of Fort Quanah lay in gray-and-black relief beneath the road. Jim saw a light in one of the buildings, and he flicked a glance at Sorrell. Sorrell's jaw toughened.

"Table's laid for company, Jim," he said. "Let's go down and pay our respects. You go first, Jim."

Jim rode down the hill and into the fort. A pack rat scurried on the ground and frightened his pony. Woodsmoke spiced the air. The glassless windows of the old orderly room were mellow with coil-oil light. Jim reined in.

"Speak up, Jim," Sorrell prompted. "No—don't dismount. I don't want you hiding behind your horse. Well, tell them we're here."

Jim pushed back his Stetson. He ran a finger over the sweat and dust on his brow. Then he confronted the small building with its splintered door. "Hello, the fort!"

He heard the rusted latch turn, and when the door opened the slender-waisted silhouette of a young woman stood there in the frame.

She was carrying a revolver.

CHAPTER 14

LAWYER FRANCIS MCKENNA'S office was on the second floor of Fowler's hotel, and one entered it from the gallery over the street. Hester visited McKenna that afternoon to beg him to make arrangements for the funeral and to ask a single legal question:

"Have I the right to manage my own affairs now?"

McKenna told her she had. He started to say more than this, but she thanked him and left. As she came onto the railed porch a man rose from a chair. He was large and bearish, with a garland of black hair clamped on his bald head and bright eyes in a face laced with lines. He wore a star, more brass than nickel, on his vest, and he had more the manner of a country doctor than of a peace officer. Sheriff Crowley laid his hat on the chair and took Hester's hand in his two hands. She had the surprising impression that he had had tears in his eyes not long before. He told her he was sorry he could not have found her before but he was out of town serving a paper.

"I just wanted to say—well, you know what I'd want to say, Miss Hester, even if I can't now. But if I can do something for you or your aunt, why, I'd feel a little better myself."

It made her want to cry, and she turned her head to look across the square at a ring of men around two cocks fighting in the dust. "If there's anything, I'll ask you. The terrible thing, to me, is that he was angry at me when he died."

"Now, don't you believe that!" the sheriff scolded. "He's been sore at me a few times, too, but the next time we'd meet we'd both have forgotten about it. Pretty soon things will be quiet again and you'll forget what it was you quarreled about."

"But that's it. In a way we're still quarreling about it. Because he thought so much of this man Harlan and I think so little."

She knew by his frown that he had heard about all the trouble. "Are you sure you're right, Hester?"

She told him how she felt about Harlan. "Well, I can't say you've poured much oil on the waters," Crowley said. "Hiring a man like Chet Anders—"

"Uncle Cam hired him, remember."

"And spent the next two years trying to figure a way to fire him without seeming ungrateful. Get rid of Chet, Hester, if you're bound to operate the ranch yourself. He'll make you nothing but trouble, and you'll get the credit."

"Do you think I'm a trouble-maker?"

Crowley smiled. "The only trouble you ever made me was when you were six years old and I was riding you around the office on my back when Governor Lew Wallace walked in!"

Just before dark Chet Anders came to Hester's hotel room to find her. He was subdued and sympathetic. He had bought himself a new jacket, and had his hair cut, and as he sat uncomfortably in a hard-backed chair in her room, with the hall door open, he said he had done what needed to be done at Paul Fleming's undertaking parlor and the funeral would be day after tomorrow. His steadiness and thoroughness comforted her.

"Miss Hester," he said, "I've been talking to Bill Holly about stepping up to the foreman's job. I think he can cut it."

"But, Chet, I was counting on you."

With a frown Anders inspected a broken finger nail. "I ain't sure it would be best."

"Why not? I don't think Bill would be half the foreman you are."

"Thing of it is," Anders said, "you and your aunt ought to agree on it, and I don't reckon Mrs. Travis cottons to me."

"Nonsense! As long as a foreman keeps the pigs out of her flower beds, she wouldn't think of criticising him."

Anders seemed relieved. "Well, it's up to you. I'd like the job fine. But I didn't want you to feel obligated or anything, and I—I kind of felt guilty about things."

"You're very good to think about it," Hester said, "but I'd be lost without you. Now, no more foolishness about quitting. I'm leaving for the ranch in a few minutes and I'd like you to go with me. We'll bring Aunt Carrie in tomorrow so she'll have a night's rest before the funeral.''

Leaving before dark, with Anders' pony trailing the buggy, they drove along the freight road. Hester pulled a kerchief over her head. Chet drove, hunched with his elbows on his knees, talking about the ranch. He wanted to sell most of the two-year-old steers.

"What's the use of feeding them after they've reached prime? We can cut them out before the roundups are finished."

Hester was not listening. She was being resentful at fate for letting a girl fall in love with a man she despised. She had enjoyed the conversation with Jim Harlan at dinner, and then had lain awake half the night remembering the things he had said to her. The deftest compliments, the warmest glances. And every one of them for a purpose! She remembered the green ink on the envelope addressed to Jim. Soon after Lovena Sorrell came to the basin, Aunt Carrie had invited her over. She had received a polite refusal in the same green ink. Hester would have given much to read Harlan's letter.

Suddenly she shivered. A cold wind hissed across the brush, cutting through her light cape. The range was lavender with early evening. Chet stopped the buggy. "Here, that won't do! Put on my jacket under your cape."

She protested, but he made her wear it. It was of heavy gray duck. He adjusted her cape over her shoulders. She saw the pleasure in his face. Men loved to see a girl wearing a garment of theirs, she thought. "My, that is better," she said. "It's a new jacket, isn't it? I haven't seen it before."

Something happened to Chet's face. It softened like wax melting in an oven. He looked absolutely stricken. His head turned slowly and he stared blindly down the road.

"What's wrong?" Hester asked.

"I shore pulled one," Chet said slowly. "I plumb left town without tending to something."

"Can't it wait?"

Chet slowly climbed down from the buggy. "I reckon not."

"You mean you're going to ride back and leave me?" she protested.

Chet wiped his mouth. "Miss Hester, I just don't have any

choice! Tell you what. The fort's just ahead. Wait there. Here, take my Colt. There won't be any trouble.''

"Do you mean to say you're going to leave me alone at night out here?''

He kept his back to her while he untied the pony. He sounded wretched. "Believe me, I'd cut off my hand to get out of this! But I—it's a promise I made another feller. I just can't let him down, Miss Hester.''

Indignantly she picked up the reins. She watched him mount. "Chet, I don't know what to think about this!''

Anders' face held the torment of a martyr on the rack. He slapped the edge of his hand against his wrist. "If this was a knife, I'd cut my hand off! I would. But I just can't do nothing but go back! I just can't!''

Whatever ailed him, he was sincere. She sighed. "All right. I'll drive on to the ranch.''

But when she reached the fort, the range was completely dark and she felt uneasy about going on. Shadows fell queerly among the ghostly old walls. She wanted to run the horse, but her practicality took command. She deliberately drove into the fort and hid the buggy in a ruined stable. She lighted a buggy lamp and walked to the old orderly room, which was used as a line shack. She carried Anders' gun with her. She would wait for Chet here. She trembled as she pushed the door.

"Is anyone here?'' The lamp fingered the trash and relics of cowboy housekeeping. She saw old magazines everywhere and horseshoes and branding irons on the walls. There was a plump lady on a coal calendar. Some cans of food on a limber-legged table gleamed. She made certain the back door was barred. Then she barred the front door and dusted a chair with a newspaper and sat down. She read some old *Harper's* articles. She studied advertisements for hair restorer, bustles, and state lotteries. At least an hour had elapsed when she heard a horse. Her spine stiffened against the chair. It was much too soon for Chet to be returning.

She moved to a corner where she could not be seen. She made herself breathe deeply. The horse came on into the fort and she heard her own horse nicker. She remembered the lamp just then, but it was too late to put it out. The gun in her hand began shaking.

"Is someone here?" a woman called.

Hester hastened to unbar the door. Outside, a girl in a dark cape sat a horse near the building. "Is it Miss Travis?" she called.

Hester put the gun behind her. "Yes. Aren't you Mrs. Sorrell?"

"Yes. I—I think I'll have to ask your help."

"Would you like to come in while you decide?"

"I don't dare come in. Someone is after me, and—"

"Is it your husband who's after you?" Hester asked.

Lovena gave a little laugh. "You do understand, don't you? I was riding to La Cinta with—with a friend—and Mr. Sorrell came after me. You see, I've left him."

"I see. Well, don't you think you'd better ride in the bosque until after he leaves? Or would it be better for you to start for home right now, as hard as you can ride?"

"No, that wouldn't do at all. Where should I hide?" Mrs. Sorrell asked.

As she returned for the lamp, Hester wondered why she should do this. She felt sure that the "friend" was Jim Harlan, and not at all sure that Mrs. Sorrell was worth saving. "Come on," she said, and hurried out.

She led Lovena on her pony to a poplar thicket. "Stay here and be quiet until I come for you," she said, and went back to wait in the orderly room. Shortly after, she heard iron shoes on the road. She picked up the Colt again, breathless, angry at Lovena for putting her in such a position. She waited beside the door until the horses halted in the yard. She heard men speaking. Then one of them called:

"Hello the fort!"

It was Jim Harlan's voice. With the lamp in one hand, the gun in the other, Hester opened the door. The horsemen were black silhouettes against a broken wall. "What do you want?" Hester asked, pointing the gun at them.

Tom Sorrell spoke first, as he removed his Stetson. "Easy, ma'am! It's Tom Sorrell and James Harlan."

She lowered the gun. "Well, what is it you want?"

"I was—I was hunting one of my men. I thought he might have stopped here."

She discerned them more clearly in the lamplight. Sorrell looked the way he used to look two years ago, before his marriage. He wore a rough cowtown coat and a gray hat curled on the sides, and his face was rude and forceful. It was as though a layer of varnish had peeled off him.

"I haven't seen your man," Hester said crisply.

"Nor anyone?" Sorrell asked.

"No one but my foreman, who had to go back to town for something he forgot. I'm waiting for him."

Jim Harlan rode forward and dismounted. "Hester, you shouldn't be out here alone," he said. "What's wrong with Anders, anyway?"

"As you see, I'm quite self-sufficient."

His eyes kept trying to ask, *Where is she?* and his hand nervously rubbed the side of his trousers. He must be fearful and ashamed. "Do you want me to stay until Anders comes back?" he asked. "I'd be obliged if you'd let me."

"Thank you, no," she observed. Harlan turned to his pony and fussed with the cinch. "Were you helping Mr. Sorrell find his man?" she asked.

"No, I'm heading for my camp. I was just riding with him. I thought I'd get a few things set up."

"So that I can knock them over?"

"I hope it won't come to that."

Sorrell handled his hat in embarrassment. "I'm very sorry about your uncle, ma'am. If there's anything I can do—"

"Don't you think you've done quite enough through the years?"

Sorrell replaced his hat. "Jim, I don't think the lady needs us," he said soberly. "Let's make her happy by leaving."

Harlan seemed to hesitate, but ended by mounting. "Good night," he told her. "Would you mind if I went to your uncle's funeral? He was a friend of mine too."

"If it pleases you."

The men rode away. Hester waited half an hour before she went down to the river to summon Mrs. Sorrell. Lovena tried to thank her, but Hester cut her off.

"Think about it," she directed, "and then tell me what you want to do—go home, or hide somewhere until Jim Harlan can get out of the basin."

"Is there anywhere I can hide?"

"In his railroad car, maybe. Or I can take you to a cabin in the foothills not far from here."

Lovena was properly humiliated. She looked down as she rode toward the fort with Hester leading her horse. "You don't think a lot of me, do you? Do you really think I was running off with him as a lover?"

"Is there any other reason a man would risk his life to help you leave your husband?" Hester asked. But she said quickly, "I'm sorry. I didn't mean to make it my business."

They rode for an hour. She installed Lovena Sorrell in an abandoned cabin in a dead orchard. She had brought all the canned food from the line shack. Now she helped her gather fuel for the fireplace.

"We've finished the fall work over here," she told the girl, "so you won't be bothered. I'll tell Jim Harlan how to find you. He'll come when it's safe, I'm sure."

Small, cold and frightened, Lovena said, "Wish me luck, Miss Travis."

Hester, adjusting the lines of the buggy with her chin up, said, "No. No, I can't. I've done everything else, but I can't wish you luck."

Lovena's lips parted. "But I don't understand! Why did you help me if you don't like me?"

"Because I don't like killings, and there would have been one if I hadn't."

The dark-eyed girl looked bewildered. "Why do you feel this way about me?"

"I don't believe it matters why I feel this way. But if you're interested, it's because—" Then she had to try to remember why she had so little affection for Lovena Sorrell. "Because we tried to make friends with you, despite how we felt about your husband, knowing you were lonesome. But you never responded. And because I feel that when a woman marries she ought to give up flirtations."

Lovena closed her lips and made a very faint smile. "Have I been flirting with someone you're trying to catch?"

Hester clenched the cold lines. "I'm not trying to catch anyone. If you mean Jim Harlan, it's gone beyond flirtation, hasn't it?"

She shook the lines and the horse left the yard. Tears obscured the road before her. Wish her luck, she thought angrily. I'll never wish either of them luck. Before heaven, I'll arm every cowboy on my ranch before I give another inch!

It seemed to Chet Anders that everybody in Divide was on the La Cinta road tonight.

Riding back to Divide, he hid under a bridge when a couple of horsemen passed. Fifteen minutes later another rider jogged by. Anders crouched in the brush with his hat over his horse's nose to keep it from nickering. He was tense as a trigger. He wished he had not given his Colt to Hester. He might need all the artillery he owned, if Sorrell had turned him in to Sheriff Crowley.

A fine, cold sweat bathed his body. Were they already after him? It would be hell to be hunted, to hide in the brush every time you heard hoofs, to be afraid to go into a new town. At last he mounted but did not return to the stage road. He sought a horse trail and followed it on toward Divide.

At last he came to the outskirts of the county seat. He wished he could be sure whether Sorrell had betrayed him. But a sliver of shrewdness ran through Anders. He knew Sorrell would rather have him as a catspaw than see him hang. He rode in by an alley, left his pony at the Home Ranch stable and told the hostler, "I'll be leaving directly. Keep him saddled."

He paced down the alley and paused outside one of the hotel windows. Through a dusty pane he scrutinized the faces of the men in the lobby. They looked normal. Anders walked into the hotel and stopped at the desk.

"Anybody been looking for me?" he asked Fowler.

"No. Reckoned you'd left, Chet."

"I had to come back for something. Loan me some writin' paper and an envelope, Joe."

He took the materials to the Gold Exchange Saloon, but every table was taken and the bar was crowded. He downed a drink and left. Finally he was forced to hold the paper against a plastered adobe wall and write his confession in the dark. He felt cold. He wished he had not given his jacket to Hester. It would be a lot colder before he got back to the ranch. He paused in his writing.

He wondered if Sorrell could make it stick. Sorrell had said he would find Anders' jacket with the horse's blood on it. He would not. Anders had torn it up on the way to town last night and dropped a rag here, a rag there, and contributed the copper buttons to the river. So Sorrell had no proof except his word—and the evidence of Anders' new jacket. But everyone knew Travis had fired Chet. It would sound reasonable. . . . But then Anders recalled the sickly faces of Death Row in the pen. No. He could not gamble. He began writing rapidly again, finished the letter and slipped it in the envelope.

He lagged toward Miller's Store, which contained the post-office. He gazed across the square toward Sorrell's upstairs room. It was dark. In the plaza the campfires of teamsters and hill farmers staying overnight burned bright. Anders actually envied the bull-whackers with their empty consciences. He reached the store and looked at the envelope. As long as I haven't mailed this, he reasoned, he'll have to prove it. The hell of it is he probably can! As long as I live, he'll hold this over me.

Tears swam to Anders' eyes. Ambition, he thought bitterly. A man worked hard and figured it all out, and what did it bring him? A hang-rope. Anders envied the late pedestrians passing up and down the walk. They knew no more about worry than a hog in a corn crib. He had an urge to get drunk. He sank back against a corner of the building.

A pebble of reason dropped almost unnoticed in his mind. Wait a minute, he thought. *Wait* a minute!

A thought appeared like a mouse from a hole. He followed it. He wet his lips, touched his jaws tenderly with his fingertips, pondering. A grin wrinkled his cheek. *Wait a minute,* he said to himself, staring at the letter in his hand. Impulsively he ripped it across. He doubled it and ripped it again. He did this until no piece remained larger than a dime. He felt drunk and wonderful. He walked briskly across the plaza, whistling. He dropped the bits of paper in a campfire where some Mexican teamsters sat eating pinto beans from a Dutch oven.

With his hands in his hip pockets, Anders paused before the bank to gaze at the upstairs room Sorrell kept. The windows were still dark. He tingled with joy. Sorrell wouldn't likely go to bed so early, so the room must be empty. No doubt he was hanging about town, perhaps waiting for Chet to drop that letter. Yet Anders opened the lower door of the tin-roofed stairway with care. He ascended and tried the upper door. It was unlocked. This made him suspicious. He let a minute run out. He opened it. The room was dark, but moonlight sketched in the rough outline of a cot, two chairs, a table, a sink with a pump at one end. Anders entered. He stood in the anemic moonlight, his eyes questing around, his feet wide-set.

"Sorrell?" he said.

He scratched a match on the wall and held his cupped hand high. Sorrell had gone out hurriedly. The cot hadn't been made and the dishes weren't washed. Anders saw the pine clothespress in one corner. His spurs chinked like stacked quarters as he crossed the room. Banked on hangers in the clothespress were pants, coats, a shortcoat, a gray horsehide jacket. The foreman wanted something which would show stains well. The horsehide jacket appealed to him. He put it on. It would look less suspicious than carrying it.

When he reached the street, he felt good. If he couldn't get enough blood out of the dead horse, he would kill one of Jacinto's goats and smear the jacket up. Then he would make a show of hiding the coat a reasonable distance from where Cam Travis had died.

As he rode from town, Anders disciplined himself into soberness. He felt grateful, and actually rather humble, at having outfoxed the fox himself.

CHAPTER 15

WHEN JIM HARLAN reached his railroad car in the cottonwood grove at Travis Siding, the night had melted like a candle, a weary, unlovely stub in a puddle of grease. He shambled into the car and found Clarence Dykes asleep in one of the beds and a note on a rosewood desk:

Hope this is okay, Jim. Mrs. Travis feeling bad. Thought I'd camp on you and get to work in the morning.

Dykes' gaunt face was blissful in sleep. Swaying, drunk with weariness, Jim gazed down. In his dreams Dykes was already working on the railroad. For ten years he had dreamed of the railroad; now he was working on it. But everyone in Magdalena Basin was taking shots at it. Sorrell didn't want it finished. Hester didn't want it started. Who the devil did want it? Jim Harlan, for a fortune. Dykes, for prestige. He would hobble down the street and people would say, "That's Clarence Dykes! He built the Magdalena-Short-Line!" Pitiful. The reasons men did things. Crazy.

Jim dropped his coat on a chair, tugged at his boots and sank back on the cot. But no crazier than Jim Harlan. Prestige. Ruby rings, tailor-made clothes, the best boots Justin ever made, with his own special last: *"Jim Harlan"* stitched on the uppers. *Think big, Jim!* Old Sullivan. Dead in a Mexican *campo santo,* dead like Jim's father. *"Git there, Jim! It don't matter how—just git there!"*

Sleep began to sift into his mind like soot shaken from a stovepipe. Suddenly he started up on one elbow. He thought he heard a girl's voice. No, a mockingbird somewhere. He had ridden for hours hunting Lovena after Sorrell left. Hester, the little minx. She knew. Give her credit for saving them, though. He dropped back and the soot began to fill his brain again, but one reflection stayed above it: I hope this isn't the night she burns the car.

Cut off her hair. A pleasure. Beautiful golden hair, bury your face in it. He pressed his face into the pillow and dreamed it was Hester's hair.

Dykes had breakfast on when Jim awoke. All through breakfast he talked railroad. "Show you how we'll bridge Grapevine Canyon!" He propped up two stiff rashers of bacon. "These are your trestles, see? All right, set her—"

Jim drank his coffee and worried about Lovena. Alone on the range, she would be like a cage bird turned loose in the forest. She ought to know how to get by, but she didn't. Too many people had done things for her. A girl to take care of, to carry across a threshold.

Dykes kept trailing him around as he nervously toured the camp. Jim would pound a couple of stakes. "We'll stack the iron here. High ground. Now, over here—" Dykes loved it. Day-before-the-circus enthusiasm shone on him like new paint. But for Jim it was a form of nail-biting, something to keep his mind off Lovena. Where was she? Would she come into camp today? If she did, they would have to move fast to get up steam and leave, for the locomotive was as cold as stone.

He walked over to where the railroad men and cowboys knelt on a tarpaulin, shooting dice. He watched the engineer roll a nine on the spread-out tarp and pull in the bets. "You'd better fire up," he told him.

"There ain't a full load of cattle yet."

"The rest may come in today. Get the ones in the corral loaded," he told the punchers.

"What if we don't take off taday? We'll have to handfeed the brutes."

"All the better if they aren't nerved up from loading when you leave. Give them time to get used to the cars."

It was shortly after this, as Jim and Dykes stood on the trestle discussing when the materials might arrive, that Dykes looked around. "Somebody coming from Muleshoe," he said.

Jim's heart jumped. He walked quickly from the trestle, looking for a girl on a sidesaddle to come in on the Muleshoe road. But it was merely Bill Holly, the range boss. He pulled up before Jim and took a wrinkled letter from his hip pocket.

"From the boss," he said regarding Jim with the unemotional, liquid eyes of a frog.

Jim studied the writing. "Miss Travis is boss now, eh?"

"Who'd you think? And Mr. Anders wants—"

"*Mister* Anders?" Jim grinned. "Who the devil is *Mister* Anders? Old Chet?"

"Do you want the message?" Holly asked.

"I didn't mean to be disrespectful," Jim said.

"He wants to know if you're going to ship these cows like you promised."

"Sure. For Cam Travis, not for Mr. Anders." Jim winked at Dykes. "I'll bet Mister Anders is sleeping in the big house, now, and taking meals with the family. I'd lay dollars to rivets he whitewashes every fence and building, too."

"Keep your eye on him," Holly said, "and maybe you'll learn something. He wants to ship some other cattle instead of the ones Travis cut out."

"Which?"

"We started cutting long yearlings this morning. There won't be any more five and sixes on this ranch. We'll have enough for herd stuff, but that'll be it from now on."

"I sure will keep my eye on him," Jim said. "I want to see how fast he can bury a going ranch."

Holly knew what he meant. "He says yearlin's will travel better than people think. And the feed lots will pay more for them than the packers."

"Maybe some day. Not now. And not over rough grades like these cattle will travel. Every steer in the car would be down and trampled. Tell Anders I won't take them."

Holly's wet, bulging eyes hardened. "Suit yourself."

Jim read the note after Holly left:

"I don't want to be classed as one of the women who write you, but you will find your lady friend in the cabin on Red's

*Meadow. Anyone can tell you where it is. But no one can tell
you how to get her to La Cinta."*

"Where's Red's Meadow?" Jim asked Dykes.

"Up near Lopez Canyon. Short ride. Why?"

It was clear in Jim's mind what had to be done, now; the sure way
and the safe way.

"I heard there might be a stand of tie-timber near there," he said.
"I don't think those cattle are coming anyway, and if they do they
can wait. Best thing would be to wait until after the funeral and ship
everything then. I'll ride up and look over that timber and then go on
to town. I'll stay there tonight and come back after the funeral
tomorrow. Day after tomorrow we'll move the cattle."

"Fine," Dykes said. "I'll go along."

"I'd rather go alone, Clancy. I want to do some thinking. You
know how it is? I'll see you before the funeral tomorrow. Then we'll
come back and hit 'er with both fists!"

Dykes showed orange vulcanite gums in a grin and smacked his
fist against his palm. "Gotcha, Jim!" Dykes loved fight talks.

Jim found the cabin, caught in the gray, arthritic arms of a
decayed orchard. He sat his pony in the yard a moment, seeing no
sign of occupancy. Then the door opened and Lovena stood there,
small and dark-haired. Suddenly she ran toward him. Jim swung
down and caught her. She was trembling.

"Oh, Jim—such a horrible night!"

He stroked her hair, uneasily glancing beyond the cabin at the
hillside which ran up to the county road. "It could have been
worse," he told her. "For a while I thought it was going to be."

She looked up at him. Her hands framed his cheeks. "You'll get
me away, Jim?"

Jim pinched her chin. "What's in it for me?"

"Me. Isn't that enough?"

She thought she meant it, Jim supposed. Maybe she did. But he
knew she would promise anything to get away. He said, "It's the
least I'd settle for."

"I'll wait for you," she said. "I'll wait forever." She drew
away. "Jim, my horse is in that gully. I'll get my things while you
saddle it."

"Wait!" He caught her wrist as she turned. "We aren't leaving today, Lovena. I'll get you day after tomorrow and you'll go up in a box car with a shipment of cattle. It's the best I can do."

She touched her cheek, shocked. "Two more nights here? Jim, I'd die! No, darling, it's got to be today. Besides, the longer I stay here, the more chance there is that I'll be found."

"Not if you stay out of sight. But if I run a one-car string up that railroad, Sorrell's going to know the kind of freight I'm carrying."

"No, Jim. I won't stay another night."

"Lovena, it can't be today!" Jim said shortly. "With people like Spurlock ranging around, you'd be seen sure."

There was a tang of wickedness in her eyes. "You're right. Perhaps Dick will find me today or tomorrow. If he does, he won't be afraid to help me. Maybe I won't even be here when you come."

Jim studied her face. "You know how to give the knife just the right twist, don't you?"

"Well, if you don't want me to go with Dick, you'd better take me yourself."

Jim was tired of arguing it. He was weary of dark roads and furtive looks over his shoulder. "It's up to you. I'm coming back day after tomorrow."

She crossed her arms, hugging herself. She smiled, but it was like a taunt. "I do hope your ride won't be for nothing."

Steadily he gazed at her. "Last night I nearly got my head blown off for you. But today you never saw me before."

Suddenly Lovena clasped his hands. "Forgive me, Jim. It just seems as though another two nights in that terrible cabin will kill me. But if you say it, I'll stay. You can kiss me, you know."

Jim kissed her. There was an emotion in him which might have been joy. He couldn't be sure. It seemed to him that the longer he lived the less he was sure of. Right now he was not even sure of himself.

He passed that night in the Home Ranch Hotel.

Cam Travis' friends gave him a lodge funeral the next morning and buried him in the community cemetery on a mesa near town. All through it, Jim watched Hester. Like her aunt, she wore a veil. She was beautiful in black. He tried to speak to her afterward but she turned her back on him. She and her aunt went to the buggy, where the minister spoke earnestly to Mrs. Travis. Jim stood awkwardly with Clarence Dykes and Day Clevis. Chet Anders came through the crowd of departing mourners. He was wearing a new black suit and gray Stetson. His jaws were shiny from soap and there was a razor nick on his chin. He had driven Hester and her aunt to the cemetery. Anders gave Jim a quick, businesslike glance.

"No hard feelings?"

"Plenty," Jim said.

"Get over them. Maybeso I can do you some good with Miss Hester. I've got nothing against railroads, so long as they treat me right."

"What's right in this case?"

"Ship those yearlin's for me. I'll make a contract with you for so many a year. Less walking they do, the more tallow they'll carry into the pens at Chicago." He had the air of a man with a cigar in his teeth and his feet on a desk. "Well, how about it?"

"I said no," Jim said.

Anders sobered. "Didn't you learn nothing the other day?"

"I learned that if you can't whip a man alone, you bring a friend the second time. I mean you're yellow as butter." Jim stood steady as Anders began to cock his fist. "Not at the boss's funeral, Mister Anders!" he said, shocked.

Anders made a snorting sound, his rough features flushing. "If you don't ship for me, you don't ship for nobody! Nobody! By damn, it looks like we still got business together, don't it?"

He walked to the buggy and drove off after taking out a cigar and lighting it.

As Jim and the others walked down the hill, Sheriff Crowley caught up with them. Dykes introduced Jim. They reminisced about Cameron Travis.

"I was out to Lopez Canyon yesterday," the sheriff said. "That is one hell of a steep slope he rolled down."

"Straight up and down," Day Clevis said.

"Seen him chase cows down steeper hills, though," Crowley said. "Done it myself, on a good horse. That Traveler horse was his favorite, wasn't it?"

"He'd a'married it, was he single."

"That's queer," Crowley said, "because he was riding Traveler when he slipped. He must have known Traveler was going to suffer, because he managed to cut its throat."

"The hell!" Dykes blurted. "Why, Cam's neck was broke, wasn't it?"

"Yes, and there was no knife around. It seemed to me like some kind-hearted feller had murdered Cam and cut the horse's throat so it wouldn't suffer."

All the men stared at him. "For reasons you can guess," the sheriff said, "I'm not spreading it around. But think about it and keep your eyes open. I'm going to spend a little time in the brush around Lopez Canyon, myself."

"Anders," Clarence Dykes whispered.

"Maybe. Maybe Tom Sorrell or Jacinto Chavez. Cam might have had a ruckus with the Mexican. I'm not going to do any guessing until I find where somebody threw his pocket-knife or buried his bloody shirt. But it gives a man something to think about."

Jim discerned a hardness like a sledgehammer in this cowtown sheriff. It was usually there in any lawman—the willingness to be brutal when it was justified. A good sheriff was a nice blend of dominie and sharpskinned hawk.

At noon Jim and Clarence Dykes started back to camp together. Dykes kept figuring reasons why the sheriff could be wrong. He had a talent for turning his face from unpleasantness. But Jim saw that he was deeply shocked.

At Travis Siding the pens were still dusty black with Muleshoe cattle. Bill Holly and a cowboy drove in late that afternoon with some hay, and Jim questioned them.

"What about these steers? Does Mrs. Travis want them sent up to La Cinta? I told her husband I'd ship them for him."

Holly broke the wires on a bale and started pitching it through the bars. "Talk to Hester about it."

"Where is she? If they're going to be in mourning over there for a week, the cars can't wait."

"She and Chet are on the way over."

Hester and Anders arrived in a dusty sunset. Hester wore a gray riding dress. She carried a quirt and held her chin high as Jim walked from the supper fire to meet her. Anders was talking to the cowboys. Jim was disturbed by the hardness in the girl.

"I'd like to ship some different cattle," she said. "The ones here will trail better than the younger ones I want to market. I can have the others here tomorrow."

"I told Anders, no. Steers that young won't travel. As like as not they'll be parked on a siding for a week and nothing but culls will ever make Chicago."

"I didn't come to you for advice," Hester said.

"But you got it, and it's better than you're getting from Anders."

"Then I won't ship these, either,"

"Suit yourself. Clevis can use the cars."

"Let him. I'd as soon not match my shipments with your whims."

She lifted the reins, but Jim caught her bridle. "Hester, I want to explain something. About the other night. I know what you thought, but the fact is—"

"Let go of my horse," Hester said.

"The fact is, Mrs. Sorrell came to me for help. I didn't ask her to leave her husband."

"For the last time," Hester said. Jim hauled the head of the horse lower. "They should make bits for hard-mouthed women," he said. "Will you get it straight that—"

Hester's quirt hissed and the leather took Jim across the face. He released the pony and put his hand to his cheek. The horse reared and he stepped back. Hester brought the horse down, her quirt still raised. Then she rode quickly up the hill to the corrals and spoke to Anders. Jim rubbed his jaw, breathless with anger. He saw Anders turn to the punchers.

"All right, let's shake it! Git off your hams and don't set them cow a-millin'! You'll start for La Cinta tonight and bed them at Medicine Spring."

"Didn't bring no chuck," one of the men said. "And we won't have these railroaders to bum off tonight."

"Cows eat grass—why not a cowboy?" Anders joked. "Come on, boys, did you hear me? Let's hit it!"

As Jim watched Hester leave, the anger ran out of him and gloom flowed in. For all her stubbornness, she had been a sweet girl. But she had determined to make a foghorn-voiced, managing sort of woman out of herself. What had Poor Richard said about whistling women and crowing hens? They would hear her whistling two counties away. She might make a first rate rancher after she got rid of Anders and his catastrophic advice, but as far as her desirability went she might as well be entering a convent.

Clarence Dykes felt the same way. At dinner he said heatedly, "She'll wind up an old maid, by damn! I declare she's going to be one of those regular ramrods of a woman! She'll have a ropin' horn bolted onto that side saddle, you watch!"

"She's sweet, though, when she wants to be," he conceded during dish-washing. "In fact I never saw her nothing but sweet, until she took on the Magdalena Railroad barehanded."

They were in bed, finally. Dykes talked railroad until his words rattled into Jim's mind like grains of corn in an empty bucket. *Narrow gauge . . . maximum radius . . . four-feet-eight-and-a-half, the U. P. . . . eighty dollars a ton trackside.*

"You can't beat a price like that now, I'll bet," he said.

"What? . . . No, I guess not," Jim said.

"When she was a little bitty thing," Dykes mused sleepily, across the dark car, "I brought her some hard candy from St. Louis. You know them little squarish ones? She said to me, 'Uncle Clancy, they look like little pillows.' Cute little kid. I wish—"

He fell asleep on the wish.

Jim wished, but could not fall asleep. He wished he could say, "Mr. Dykes, I've got another face I want to show you. It's the one I wear when I'm talking to Mart Rawling, of Great Southern, my boss. Yes, my boss. It goes way back, why I had to run this sandy on you people. My dad—never mind. I didn't figure it would hurt anybody—"

A brain should be made like a pigeonhole desk. Then you could slip your worries into a small square pocket until you were ready for them. Jim's brain was like a silo full of trash, and he was at the bottom of it trying to fight his way out. At length he fell asleep.

He did not sleep long, however. He heard a thud under the car. Then a surging orange light illuminated the bedroom. Dykes was sitting up in bed. Jim smelled coal oil and burning paint. Horses were running. Jim rolled out of bed and jammed his feet into his boots. He tried to decide what to save: The papers? His clothes?

"Holy smokes, Jim!" Dykes shouted. "We're on fire!"

"Get your plans, Clancy," Jim told him. "This thing will go up like straw."

The flames had mated in ecstasy with the varnish, paint, and oak. Jim and Dykes salvaged some clothing, the strongbox, and a little food.

Then the windows of the bedroom burst inward and the night bulged with a gigantic stutter of rifle fire. Jim groped on the floor for a break in the shots that swept up and down the car. All the firing was coming from the stream bed.

Seated on the floor, Dykes was trying to cock a leveraction repeater. Jim took it from him and gave him his Colt. A bullet crashed through a stained glass transom.

Jim laid the rifle barrel over a jagged sill and tried to see beyond the trees. His eyes picked up a few flashes and then the flames sweeping across the window blinded him. He fired three shots and crouched again. Smoke was leaking through the warping planks.

"Jim, Jim!" Dykes wheezed. "We got to get out of here, boy. My asthma—"

A new gun crashed from the direction of the locomotive. Another began to speak with it, and at once the fire in the stream bed ceased. The railroad crew had got organized. Jim and Dykes carried a few things out and took refuge on a flat car of supplies. In the night, horses began to run. Jim worked over to the river bank. The arroyo was empty. Firelight reddened the small stream in the middle of the wash. He ran back to the car called *Rio Arriba*. Standing there in pants, boots and underwear, rifle trailing from his fingers, he heard the trainmen asking what under the sun had happened. Was this a stray Mexican revolution or something?

"It's nothing," Jim told them. "Miss Hester decided to throw a little barbecue, is all."

He saddled his horse and slid the carbine under the stirrup. "Where to, Jim?" Dykes asked.

"Over to Muleshoe," Jim said. "I made Hester a promise I've got to keep."

Dykes' sunken features were all firelight and shadow. "You ain't going to back out, Jim? We're still going to build the railroad, ain't we?''

''This is the best reason yet why we've got to build the railroad.''

Riding to Muleshoe, Jim Harlan did some calculating.

Hester would know she and the men might be followed. Probably she would ride down Iron Creek for a good distance, since it offered fast travel in a false direction. Then they could cut due east and be back at the ranch. But the shortest way was by the wagon road Hester had driven the other day. It was easy to follow in the failing moonlight, and Jim kept his horse at a scuffing trot and stared straight ahead. In his pocket he carried a pair of shears from his bachelor's sewing kit.

Muleshoe headquarters lay in a covey of cottonwoods and black-walnut trees at the base of a long mesa. Jim halted in the trees. He familiarized himself with the layout. The barns and corrals were grouped off to the right. The main house loomed directly before him. It seemed to be constructed in an open square arrangement, with a walled patio in the center. Jim could see an arched gate in it. All the windows were dark. He rode around the left side of the building. The bunkhouse stood in the rear, behind some sheds and a chicken yard. He saw a high pole in the chicken yard with an owl trap atop it. Outside a door in the corner of the building was a chopping block and a woodpile.

On Iron Creek, now, the beautiful car he had been so proud of would be a sprawl of red ashes. Anders would make jokes about it as the Muleshoe men rode home with Hester, and they would all laugh heartily because he was the boss, now, really the boss, excusing a couple of women. Jim turned the horse briskly into the brush on the side of the mesa and found a place to leave it. He left his spurs hanging by the chains from the saddle-horn.

He walked quietly to the front of the house and tested the gate. The rawhide hinges swung silently. Jim entered a small garden with a walk leading to a veranda. Rose bushes stood in neat, dispirited rows, and a trumpet vine climbed a wall, its fragrance heavy as cheap perfume. The house had a second story across the rear but the wings were of single height. The logical place to wait, he supposed, was where he would be hidden by the gate when it opened—assuming Hester did not come in by the kitchen door.

He squatted down and trimmed his nails for a long time with the shears. The stars began to fade. He saw a mouse creep along a walk. He heard an insect ticking in the corner. A soft flutter of hoof-beats came from the west. The horses came through the trees at a walk. Jim rose and put his back to the wall. Harness clinking, a file of horses halted before the gate.

"Take Miss Hester's horse," Anders voice said. "I'll be along directly. And be quiet. Mrs. Travis may not have woke up. She needs her sleep."

The horses moved off.

"It's all right, Chet—just leave me here," Hester said. "Better not risk waking Aunt Carrie. It's a blessing if she can sleep at all."

The gate opened and Jim drew his gun. He yearned for the delicious chop of the barrell through Ander's Stetson.

"Whatever you say," Anders agreed. His voice sounded rough but affectionate. "You're a real good scout, Hester. I'll make a hand out of you yet."

"Oh, I'll be tying my own steers in a month." The girl laughed.

"Not while Chet's around to do it for you."

"You are my man Friday, aren't you? And I'm glad I stayed back, as you told me. One of their bullets might have hit me."

"By George, if it had . . . !"

You stupid ox, Jim thought. You hog in spats. Get back to the bunkhouse and moon over the girl on the liver-pill calendar.

"You're sure none of your shots hit anyone?" Hester asked.

"Oh, no! No, no. We shot high so's they wouldn't."

About eye-level, Jim recalled. For an instant his leg muscles tensed, and he almost walked out the gate to say, Down on your face, Prince Charming. I'll take the lady from here.

Hester paused in the arch of the gate. "Good night, Chet. I hope we taught him a lesson."

"Don't worry about that." Then a smile entered Anders' voice, a smile and an awkwardness. "If I weren't such a gentleman, I'd take a kiss for the night's work."

"Well, we don't want anyone but gentlemen around here, do we?" Hester said.

Good, Jim thought. Good! But then she said, "But just so you can be a gentleman and not suffer for your chivalry—"

He heard her kiss him, and it rocked him like a stone between the eyes. He imagined her Swiss-watch daintiness in the foreman's hands, and felt a curious flash of resentment. If a girl like that will kiss a man like Anders, you can't trust any girl in the world, he thought. He heard Anders call, "Hester!" but she came through the gate, calling a soft good night as she closed it. She dropped the horseshoe latch in place and turned up the walk.

Jim's hand went over her mouth. He heard the quick draw of her breath between his fingers. Then she slumped and he had to support her. He went sick with fear. He had heard of people dying of seizures when they were surprised. He held her with an arm about her waist, but kept the other hand lightly over her mouth. In a moment she began to move. She threshed in his arms and her boots scuffed the gravel. She fought as if she had gone insane.

"Easy!" Jim said. "Be a good scout for me, too, Miss Hester. This is old Jim Harlan."

She stopped fighting then. Her breathing was spasmodic. "I brought along a wad of grease-waste for a gag," Jim said. "I won't use it if you'll promise to be quiet, but otherwise I'll have to choke you down while I rig it up."

He loosed his hand a trifle. "What do you want?" she asked.

"I want my car back. Car like that costs twenty-thirty thousand dollars. I had all my things in it—everything but the clothes I'm wearing. All my pictures of my folks. My letters."

"You know, I warned you."

"I warned you, too. Let's go down the road and get to it."

Her hands went to her hair, in swift recollection. *"No!* You wouldn't!"

"Snip-snip." Jim shrugged. "Easy as that."

He had to muffle her then, but when he moved his hand to her throat and sighed, "Reckon I've got to do it," she ceased struggling. They passed through the gate and over the bare ground to the wagon road. As he led her up the road, Jim glanced down at her.

"You sure look foolish dressed like a she-cowboy. What's a hen want to be a rooster for?"

"To protect what belongs to her."

"Being pretty belongs to you too, doesn't it? What's pretty about clothes like that? Bet you got rope burns, too. Anders teaching you to rope?''

He stopped and led her under a tree and put her back to it. He placed one hand on either side of her against the trunk, imprisoning her there while he grinned at her.

"He's—he's taking my side in the fight, of course."

"You didn't give him much fight over that kiss, did you?"

He could see some tears on her cheeks but her eyes held steady. Her mouth was sober and very prettily shaped. She was not merely pretty. She was beautiful—and sweet and sincere. But she shot and burned railroad cars and quirted her enemies.

"Why shouldn't I kiss him if I like him?"

"*Like* him! Nobody likes Anders, do they? He's just something you have to put up with, like mosquitoes."

"Does he seem that way to you?" Her lips suggested a smile. "I find him quite attractive."

Jim pulled the shears from his hip pocket and clicked them beside her head. "Think Anders will find you attractive tomorrow?"

Her chin puckered. He knew she was going to cry. "I've been twenty years growing that hair!"

"Then by the time you're forty you'll have it back again. Of course it may be gray—"

Suddenly she ducked out of his arms. Jim caught her by one wrist and yanked her back. She fought with her fingers, her boots, her knees, but he wrapped her in his arms and crushed the breath out of her, and while she sobbed he freed his right hand and began cutting. He heard the fine golden hair part like silk. A heavy swatch of it fell to the ground. Hester began sobbing.

"Oh, oh, oh!" she wailed.

Jim gazed at the beautiful braid of hair on the ground and was shocked. But he set his jaw and started to cut again. She struggled so fiercely that he had to drop the scissors to avoid cutting her. Again he locked her in his arms. The top of her head pressed against his face. Her hair was warm and fragrant. They struggled together and Jim pushed her back against the tree. She stopped fighting. He could bend and retrieve the shears, now, but he didn't. He held her closely, his fingers digging the softness of her shoulder.

Then he heard her gasp. "Are you punishing me, Jim, or making love to me?"

He leaned back to look at her face. Her lips were parted. Suddenly he kissed them. Then he kissed her hair and throat, and as suddenly as spring rain she began to cry. Her arms raised and went about him, and Jim kissed her mouth so hard their teeth touched. His ardor grew savage. There was no frontier between his desire and his strength. He felt her trembling.

At last he freed her. It was like unlocking a huge and heavy door to let his arms fall. She stood before him with beauty on her like a sunrise. There was beauty within her, and in her eyes. "What is it, Jim?" she whispered. "What is it, dear?"

And he thought, This is where it falls apart, the good fast life—this is where they collect from you. When you want a girl like this and you're not good enough for her.

He stooped and picked up the golden braid from the ground. He felt tired. He was going to give the braid back to her. But he knew he was too far along this road to turn back. He had to go on. He coiled it around his hand and put it into the pocket of his coat.

She did not understand what he was doing. Her eyes watched every move he made, and she had the expression of a girl waiting for something wonderful to happen. She said, "You don't have to cut it off, if you want it. You can have all of it." She pulled some pins from her hair and it all slipped down about her shoulders.

Jim turned away. He gazed up the road. "If you block me again," he said, "I will take all of it. I don't like to be rough. But—you know I mean it now."

He left her there. It seemed cruel and treacherous, but she would know before long why he had done it. There was a lot in her head besides dreams of lovely things to wear. She would figure him out, and know for sure that Jim Harlan was as false as a pewter wedding ring.

The sun slanted over a mountain and caught Jim short of Travis Siding. He rode in while the men were eating breakfast. He slumped onto a pile of ties beside the fire and a man put a tin cup of coffee in his hand. Jim drank it.

"What'd you do over there?" Dykes asked.

"Kept a promise," Jim said. He pulled the braid from his pocket and showed them, but he felt sick when he looked at it.

"Holy cow, Jim!" Dykes said.

The firemen took the tawny braid from Jim with a chuckle. He lifted his striped trainman's cap and looped the hair on top of his head. "Who'd like the next dance?" he asked.

"Give that here," Jim snapped. White with anger, he snatched it away, staring at the fireman.

"Okay! What the hell? You cut it off, didn't you?"

"Yes, but that was—forget it. Have you started unloading that boxcar yet?"

"Near finished."

"Finish it early. Clevis will be here with his cattle this morning and that car goes with it."

"What's the idea?" Dykes asked him. "You'll be putting your ironware out in the weather."

"No other choice."

Jim walked to the river and kicked rocks into the water. It was a cold morning. He saw trout jumping downstream. Ought to take a gray hackle, he thought. Hook a mess of ten-inchers in fifteen minutes. He put his hand in his pocket and held the thick plait of hair. There was no way out of this snakepit except backwards, and backwards would leave Tom Sorrell in command.

He knew he should start for Lovena soon. He wanted her to be here, ready to leave, the minute the cattle cars were loaded. About nine he decided to go after Lovena. The dust of Clevis' cattle had been sighted down the valley. He took Dykes aside.

"Right up some kind of bed in that boxcar, will you? Somebody's going up to La Cinta with the cattle."

He crossed the stream and rode up the long, eroded tilt of range toward the cabin where Lovena was hidden. He went cautiously, coming up out of an arroyo some distance south of the cabin to cut sign before he went any closer. He could see on the hillside the gray blue of dead fruit trees which hid the cabin. Jim was on the point of riding on when he saw three horsemen on the La Cinta road, which followed a ridge behind the cabin. It seemed to him that they were watching him. One of them put a hand on the brim of his Stetson. By the gesture, Jim knew him. It was Dick Spurlock.

He was so near the cabin that Spurlock could not fail to make the connection. Yet he knew he must try to throw them off. He dismounted and walked some distance from the horse. He tried to think how a location man did it when he was taking a sighting. He framed his hands in a box and peered across the valley. Then he made a small pyramid of stones for a corner and walked back to the horse.

He rode south and cut into the arroyo again.

When he came back half-an-hour later, the riders were gone. But as he rode closer he saw a man lying on a flat boulder beside the road, smoking as he lounged on one elbow. Spurlock had hidden his horse out of sight. Jim thought bitterly, He should have been an Indian. He could steal fresh meat from a cougar.

Spurlock threw his smoke away and made Jim a hat-signal to stay where he was. He rode down the slope. They met on the bank of a wash. Spurlock's raw nature showed in his face.

"Lost?" he asked Jim. "Your camp's yonderly."

"No, I'm not lost," Jim said. "Why didn't you bring your friends?"

"I told them you saw us." Spurlock smiled. "Why'd you pile up the rocks?"

"I like piling rocks. They wouldn't let me do it as a kid."

"Where is she?" Spurlock demanded.

"Probably in Cincinnati, by now. You should know. Didn't she tell you where she was going when she left?"

"Now, listen——" Spurlock began, crowding forward.

"No, you listen. I'm sending some cattle up to La Cinta, and I'm busy. If you need to know something, ask it, but let's get off this track before we have trouble."

Spurlock's lips looked dry. His skin was so sallow that his freckles stood out.

"You think you're going to smuggle her out and have her for yourself, don't you? But do you know what she said when she asked me to help her get away from the ranch? She said you didn't mean a damned thing to her—she just needed you for a ticket! I think she's got some guy in the East."

"She's got some guy everyplace," Jim said sadly. "Some lonesome railroad builder, some ramrod—and she's faithful to them all. Because none of us means anything to her, and that includes pussyfooting foremen like you. She doesn't need a man. She needs men.''

Spurlock crowded his horse into Jim's and slugged at his head. Jim caught his wrist and twisted it. Their faces came close, and he kept twisting. Spurlock cocked his other fist but did not throw it because he knew Jim would break his wrist.

"Don't heat yourself," Jim said. "You're drunk on her, and you've got to sober up. She's not for cowhands, Spurlock. Sorrell's got more than you'll ever have, including money, and look at him!''

"Sorrell's a—'' Spurlock gritted his teeth.

"He's her husband. Keep telling yourself that.''

"She's left him! He won't be her husband long.''

"But you'll never be. So ease out of it before you get in trouble.''

Spurlock's pony backed. The ramrod gazed at Jim as if he had discovered something in him that made him want to make friends. In his stiff way, he looked as though he might break down.

"Are you in love with her or not, Harlan? You don't sound it.''

"You tell me. You think *you're* confused. Some day I'll tell you my troubles.''

"Tell me now,'' Spurlock invited, with a grin.

"Then I really would have trouble,'' Jim said.

He rode away. Now he knew there was no possibility of bringing her from the cabin today. Tonight he would try to get her to the siding and tomorrow they could take off early. But he was afraid to try to move her far by road.

He told the train crew they would not be taking the boxcar after all. "Kick it onto the siding. Maybe tomorrow.''

"What are you going to use for an engine tomorrow?'' the engineer asked. "This one goes with us to Albuquerque.''

It stopped Jim for a moment. The cars were loaded with bawling steers which had to be moved. He said finally, "I'll need a work engine anyway until my own outfit gets here. Maybe I can promote one at La Cinta today. I'll go up with you.''

With a string of slatted cattle cars, a cowboy on each car to watch for down cattle, they pulled from Travis Siding. Jim settled down to a serious game of poker in the caboose with the brakeman and a switchman.

CHAPTER 16

ANDERS WAS too full of romance to sleep after the kiss Hester gave him. The bunkhouse pulsated with snoring and sweat-smells. In one of the pictures in his mind he was sleeping in the main bedroom and Hester was by his side—his wife, now. Chet Anders, boss of the whole layout! He tried out names for the special breed of Brahma, whiteface, and Angus he would develop. The Magdalena Strain. Braeford. Somebody already had that. Bragus. Angford. He went to sleep designing a new brand for this special herd.

In the morning he and Hester went over some ranch business in the office. Someone rode into the yard. Anders showed Hester how many yearlings they could afford to sell without jeopardizing the herd. Hester tried to understand it. He patted her head.

"You'll catch on, missy." And then, because women like you to notice every little change they made in themselves, he said, "Something different about your hair, ain't there?"

Hester blushed and touched the right side of her hair. "A little. I've done it the old way so long—"

Bill Holly came to the door. "Beg pardon, Miss Hester—man to see Chet."

"Who is it?" Anders growled.

"Dick Spurlock."

A cold finger slid down Anders' chest. Spurlock equaled Sorrell. What did Sorrell want? Pressure already?

"Won't take a minute," he told Hester. He put the pencil over his ear and sauntered out.

Anders found Spurlock waiting by the concrete water tank in the

122

yard. With one leg cocked across the swell of his saddle, Spurlock was spinning the rowel of his spur. "Boss wants you."

Anders felt a flood of anger break loose in him. This big-ranch ramrod talking down to the little-ranch ramrod! "Whose boss is that?" he asked.

"Mine. He's over to Fort Quanah. We're taking a pasear. Wants you to go along."

The hell with him, Anders thought. But relations between him and Tom Sorrell had not been established yet. He would have to play it carefully until they found the bloody jacket in the brush.

"I'm busy," Chet said. "Tell him—"

Spurlock began to smile. "Tell him what?"

"Five minutes," Anders said.

It was the first cold fall day the basin had had. Tom Sorrell had a pot of coffee simmering over a fire tucked into a corner of a roofless building when they arrived. It was now about ten o'clock, but the sun was pale yellow. With his back to them, Sorrell squatted before the fire, a tin cup in his hand. His Stetson rested on the back of his head. He did not look around, and as he spoke his voice sounded to Anders like the burlap baritone of a whiskey-fighter.

"Take a ride, Dick."

Spurlock swerved his pony away, leaving Anders to stare at the rancher's back, as nervous as a sparrow in a parlor. He had Sorrell in his pocket, but he didn't have. Sorrell was fast, powerful and treacherous. He reminded Anders of some men in the penitentiary. Even in solitary they made you jumpy.

"What's the trouble, Mr. Sorrell?" he asked.

"Got anything against dumping trains in canyons, Chet?"

Anders' nerves eased out. "Well, I almost had a go at dumping one the other day, but Harlan came along too soon."

"If you'd succeeded," Sorrell said, "I'd probably have drowned you in sheep dip. I've gone to a lot of trouble setting that man up in business here."

"*You* set him up?" Anders pushed his hat back.

Sorrell stood up. Anders could see that he had not shaved in several days. His mouth pulled down at the corners and his eyes were sour and cynical. He looked like a well-to-do cowman just back from a prolonged tour of the El Paso pleasure palaces.

"I've got an interest in his railroad," Sorrell said. "I was going to operate it on the quiet, but now he's making sounds like an empire builder and refusing to work with me. I've given him his chances. Now I'm going to let him know I'm firing real bullets." He paused. "Those cows of Day Clevis' aren't going to get to La Cinta today."

"Why tell me about it?"

"Because I don't want to be too close to the firing line. I'll show you and Dick how I want it set up, but you'll do the work. Got it?"

Anders' hand fingered the concho on the lanyard of his Stetson. "You really meant it, eh? That you'd want a favor done."

"I'm not asking you to kill anybody. And it seems as if you don't even draw the line there."

"Somebody *could* be killed in a wreck," Anders said.

"Risks in all trades," said Sorrell. "The hell with talking about it. Are you in it, or not?"

"Let's go," Anders said evenly.

They overtook Dick Spurlock a short distance up the county road. The wind strengthened, hissing in the telegraph wire beside the road and fluttering the raveled threads of the blades of the Spanish bayonnet.

Not far from the old Shelton place, Spurlock spotted a rider below them. Anders, who had good vision, could scarcely make the horseman out, but Spurlock had an eye like a buzzard.

"Who is it?" Sorrell asked quickly.

Spurlock curled the brim of his hat and studied. "Can't say. Might be Sheriff Crowley."

"Damn it!" Sorrell said.

"Don't reckon he's seen us," Spurlock said. "Why don't you ride along? I'll get a line on him. If it's Crowley I'll tell you, and we'd better give it up."

Sorrell and Anders rode ahead. An hour later, Dick Spurlock caught up. "It was just that old lunatic, Dykes."

Anders laid a careful gaze on him. Spurlock looked stiff and preoccupied. Anders had the feeling his mind had slipped its hobbles, that he couldn't focus on the business at hand. Spurlock was a queer one.

"All right, look here." Sorrell had drawn rein at the edge of a mesa which fell by stairsteps of rimrock to a canyon bottom. Across the canyon mounted a higher mesa with some small timber along its crest. Anders looked down and began to smile. Below, he saw the tracks of the short line and a little trestle where they vaulted the deep, dry bed of the canyon, jumping from the foot of the nigh mesa to the slope of the far one. It was the same bridge he and Hester had been working on when Harlan arrived!

He heard Sorrell saying almost the same things he had said to Hester. "It won't take much to kick a rail loose. The engine will pitch over the side and take half the cars with it."

"What happens to the crew?"

"Maybe they're quick on their feet," Sorrell speculated. "Let them worry about it. They didn't have to work with Harlan, did they?"

"No, sir," Anders agreed.

"All right, get started. Leave your horses here. If you hurry you'll be back up here before they come. Either way, they'll be too busy to see you."

Sorrell carried a crowbar in his rifle scabbard. He handed it to Anders. Dick Spurlock carried a carbine as they descended the high rimrock stairs. The cold wind swept up from the canyon. Yellowing grasses sweetened the air. Rills of small stones rattled down the hill from their boots. They reached the stream bed, crossed the sand and climbed to the tracks on the opposite hillside. Spurlock picked the rails they would move, one on each track so that the effect would be that of an open switch. Anders put his brawn to the work of pulling spikes. They teamed up to bend the rails. Completed, the job was creditable. The rails, Anders guessed, would lead that locomotive by the nose right into the wash.

"Let's go," Spurlock growled. As they were crossing the sand he raised two fingers warningly.

"What?"

"Whistle," Spurlock said. "Come on."

Half way up the slope, Anders heard the whistle and the chuff of pistons. He reached the top, out of breath and excited. He had an impulse to get out of sight, because there was going to be pure hell here, with the train crew dumped down the rocks among a hundred odd steers and live steam exploding like cannon shells.

Spurlock was wedging himself in a deep crack in a ledge of black rimrock. "What the hell you doin'?" Anders asked.

Spurlock cocked his rifle and sighted down the browned barrel. "In case we miss fire," he said.

"Who you gunnin' for? Harlan?"

"The boiler jacket, in case they stop in time."

"You're a liar," Anders said. "You're gunning for somebody. You come on, or somebody's going to see you."

"Dick!" Sorrell shouted from the top of the mesa. "Get up here, dammit!"

Spurlock did not turn his head. The sound of the train was closer. Anders began to climb rapidly, swearing. That everlastin' damned Apache, he thought, would put ants in his grandmother's ear trumpet!

Jim had been losing money to the trainmen ever since they left Travis Siding. On his knees on the trashy floor of the caboose, among crusts of old sandwiches and the corpses of dead cigars and cigarettes, he watched the cards flutter down for a new hand. He picked them up and sorted nothing above an eight. The brakeman rubbed a greasy finger against his nose.

"Shoot a buck," he said.

"A buck!" the switchman said. "Who we playin' against, Jim—John Jacob O'Flaherty?"

Jim covered and took five cards. You could not win that way, but he had the feeling, Maybe I'll burn out my bad luck here. His luck had to change sometime. But actually it didn't. It had never changed for Harlan Senior.

He drew a pair of treys.

"Jim, you ain't doin' so good," the brakeman observed. He shuffled. "Cards," he murmured. "Let's make 'em all red this time. Red is the color of my true love's hair."

Forward there was a loud thumping like a pile of ties collapsing, a whistle blast like a scream. The brakeman's eyes met Jim's. All of them started to rise, then all lurched foolishly against the side of the car. A crash of pans reverberated in the galley. The car stumbled and righted itself. The men struggled up and scrambled for the rear platform. The whistle was blowing. It ended in a gurgle. A tremendous sound of escaping and clattering metal echoed in the canyon. From the cattle cars rose a wild chorus to lift goose-flesh on a man's arms. The caboose tilted again and Jim knew it was going all the way this time.

The drop hurled him against the cupola ladder and he wrapped his arm and legs about it. The car jolted against the earth with a splintering roar. Jim felt the skin tear on his palms as he hung onto the iron ladder. Now he was upside down in a squirrel cage of flying pillows, blankets, tools and lanterns. Glassware shattered in bright bursts of sound, wood ripped down the grain and men bawled loudly in despair. Jim's brain turned off like a lamp. He hung onto the ladder. That was all he needed to think about and all there was to think about.

Then motion stopped. It was so still that he wanted to scream to break it. Because this was the wrong sort of stillness, the sort which blew up like a cannon and tore you apart with the horrible sounds it had been holding in. He rolled away from the ladder and staggered out through long sabers of varnished wood. He leaped from the platform but sat down on the sand, looking up at the flattened caboose.

Yonder, beneath the bridge, a man was screaming as tirelessly as a baby. He would scream as long and loud as he could, then he would fill his lungs and scream again. Another man was saying, "Ed, Now, Ed!" Stunned, not thinking yet, Jim sat there. His neck was limber. It would not quite support his head as he gazed around the canyon bottom. Cattle were struggling, bawling, bleeding. Dirty gray steam drifted from the ruined locomotive and the smell of hot oil and rust tainted the air.

The scene looked like a battlefield on which the soldiers had been red-uniformed steers. The brakeman lay doubled across a rock. He still held some cards in his hands and one of his boots was off. Cowboys were staggering around in the brush. The switchman was crawling on the sand. Somebody better help him, Jim thought. He got to his feet deliberately, like a drunkard proud of being able to stand up. Then something smashed into an iron truck at his feet and a thin, spiteful cry snapped at him.

It seemed as if a window opened to clear his brain. He knew the sound of the caroming bullet and he followed the sound toward its source. A second bullet struck near him and he ran his eyes up the dark rimrocked wall across the wash. Smoke whipped from a cleft of rocks.

He lunged for the caboose. Standing in the doorway, he looked around in that stew of broken things for the company rifle. He saw it finally in a litter of blankets. He picked his way to it. Coming out, he glanced about the wash until he saw where he wanted to be—a big watermarked rock at the foot of the slope. He limped to it. A bullet passed him and etched a shining streak of silver on the rock. Jim dropped behind it and examined the gun. It was a Henry. It was probably as dirty as an Army cook's rifle, but perhaps it would shoot straight.

High up on the wall of the mesa, a man rose cautiously with his carbine lowered. Jim snapped the forty-four to his cheek. He put his shoulder against the rock and aimed. The front sight rose and fell with his breathing. He held his breath. He fired and saw dust kick up twenty-feet below the sniper. The man went down into the rocks.

Jim dug his boots into the sand. He kept filling his lungs. He brushed what he thought was a strand of hair from his eyes, and saw blood on his hand. He took a bead on the sniper's perch. A dark head came up and ducked down, and he caught the flash of a gunbarrel. The pale slant of a cheek appeared and remained. The gunman was taking aim. Jim's rifle jolted his shoulder. He knew instantly he had made a hit, knew it from the way the gun felt. He saw the rifleman's gun lurch. Jim cocked and aimed but waited while an arm appeared and the gun went sliding down the rocks. Then he saw a man try to climb out of a wedge in the rimrock, propping himself up with both arms. He lined his sights on the center of the sniper's chest, and just before he fired he realized that it was Dick Spurlock. The Henry jumped in his hands and Spurlock collapsed. He fell forward and hung there, half out of the rocks.

In the wash, escaping steam from the locomotive, continued its angry hiss. Among the injured cattle, cowboys were beginning to move around. Jim felt completely drained. He let the rifle fall and slumped back against the rock. Numbly, he gazed at the blood and destruction. It was like a city which had been blasted by artillery. Harlanville, he thought: built by a man who had to get there, no matter how. As he looked he felt the tears fill his eyes.

There had been a telegraph key on the train. One of the trainmen carried it up to the telegraph line and sent word to Divide. The news went by foot to nearby ranches, and one of the wagons which arrived late that afternoon was driven by Chet Anders. Bill Holly rode with him.

In the canyon, quiet efficiency reigned. Seven men, too badly injured to ride, were laid on hay in the wagons and covered with blankets. The engineer had been scalded to death by live steam. The brakeman had been crushed in the wreck.

Clarence Dykes, who had come up early, thought they should bring Spurlock's body down from the cliff. But Jim said, "Let the dead bury their dead."

"Do you think Sorrell set him to do it?"

"If I can prove it, Sorrell will be as dead as Spurlock," Jim said. "Clancy, I've got to tell you something."

"I'm listening," Dykes said, after a moment.

"Never mind," Jim did not have enough energy to confess. Tomorrow he would clear his decks and do what they wanted him to, which he supposed would be to pull out. But he had to make it plain that there had been two dogs in the Magdalena manger, and the big one would still be left.

So in the dusk they left the place and started for Divide. Doc Watkins drove out in his buggy and met them on the road. He set two broken legs and an arm before they came to Divide, in the frosty heart of the night. Everyone in town seemed to be up. Many had ridden out to meet the wagons. They brought Jim their condolences and he had nothing to say but thanks. He still had his room at the Home Ranch. He limped to it on the sprained ankle Watkins had wrapped. He closed the door without lighting the lamp and started to unbutton his shirt. But he was too exhausted to undress. He sat on the bed, fell back and closed his eyes.

CHAPTER 17

HIS WATCH said eleven o'clock when he awoke. He lay on the bed with his arm across his face. This was the day to accomplish so much, but all he wanted was to drown himself in sleep. It was the day to tell Divide why he had come here; to try to explain that something had changed so that he no longer felt as he had. It was also the day to confront Tom Sorrell with what he believed and try to read him. If he read Sorrell plainly, if there were no doubt in his mind, he would kill him.

The Mexican with the dusty hair came to his room with a pitcher of hot water. "The senor desires hot water?"

"Thanks." Jim saw something in the black-enamel eyes. "What's the matter?"

"There is nothing the matter." The Mexican touched his forehead and moved away.

Jim closed the door, frowning. He was halfway through shaving when Clarence Dykes entered.

"Bother you if I set down?" Dykes asked. He was dressed the way he had been dressed when Jim first met him, in funeral black and with his corded neck centered in a collar big enough for a draft horse. He was very sober.

"Don't be formal," Jim said. He saw Dykes in the mirror as he shaved. The old man looked ill. Dykes took an onion-skin paper from his pocket.

"This was in my box this morning," he said. "Clevis got one, too, and 'most everybody I've talked to. It's from Tom Sorrell."

Jim's hand jerked. A tiny cut opened on his chin. He put a corner of the towel to it. "What's on his mind?"

"I'll read it." Dykes put on his spectacles, but immediately removed them. "Ah, I can't read it! I haven't been so upset since my wife died. Listen, Jim. He says you're working for Great Southern, and when you're finished you'll sell the road to them. Is that true?"

Jim wiped his face and sat by the old man. "Clancy, it's as true as a plumb-bob. That's my game—building railroads for what I can milk out of them. But it was always down in Mexico before, and it seemed different. That is, I didn't get so involved with people down there. It was done for the government, and it had more risks than seven cases of dynamite. The man I was working with got shot, for instance."

"You'll probably get shot here," Dykes said.

"I'll risk that, if I get to speak my piece first. I'm going to speak it to you right now, and then tackle the others. You remember that little speech you made to me about an engineer needing to build railroads, like a clock needs to tick? Well, that's the way I've needed something too, only it's not easy to explain what it is I've needed. Maybe it was prestige—but it took the form of money. I come from poor folks. Good but poor. Good and poor usually go together. Ever noticed?"

"Can't say as I have."

"Take yourself. You're good and skilled at your trade, but you're stalled."

"That's my fault, not anybody else's. I could have gone out looking for a job, but I was stubborn and hung onto this thing. Just to prove I was right. It was a buildable road and I was going to build it."

Jim stood up. "You still can."

"For Great Southern? I wouldn't lay them track enough to roll a perambulator across the street."

"For yourself! For you and Clevis and Hester—the whole bunch of you! But mostly yourself, because you're going to be the engineer and the one the finances revolve around."

Dykes' eyes roved the baseboard of the walls. Wordlessly he shook his head.

''What about your coal interests? Somewhere there's a banker—
and I'll find him—who can see that all that stands between you and a
fortune is a railroad. He'll put up part of money for the railroad and
others will put up the rest. In a year you'll be taking coal out of the
San Pedros.''

Dykes' enthusiasm was slow and damp. ''I doubt that,'' he said.
''I doubt that.''

''Why?''

Dykes made a cynical smile. ''If there was any money in it, Tom
Sorrell would have taken it away from me before now.''

''Ah!'' Jim said. ''Now we're getting there!'' He told the old
man the story. It was hard to know whether Dykes was listening, or
whether he believed it at all. Dykes was insulated from the world.

''It's the truth, Clancy,'' Jim said earnestly.

''You've been lying to me for a week,'' Dykes told him. ''You
went to Cam Travis' funeral as a liar. You gave Hester pious hell
when she spotted you for what you were. What makes you any
better than Tom Sorrell?''

''I'm not a murderer. That's one thing that makes me better.
Either Sorrell or Anders helped Spurlock dump our train today, and
one of them killed Travis!''

''Want to say that to Anders?'' Dykes asked.

''Where is he?''

''At the Gold Exchange. They're talking over what to do about
you. Whole gang's there, everybody but Sheriff Crowley. He took a
posse out to search the canyon where the train was wrecked. Why
don't you go down and say it to Sorrell?''

Jim took his Colt from the back of a chair and buckled it on. But
as he glanced down at it, the gun seemed in bad taste. He was going
out to do penance, to make his manners. The gun said, *And if you
don't forgive me, I'll kill you!* He hung it over the chair again.

''There isn't a thing a Colt can say that I can't. I'm on my own
this time.''

''I reckon you are,'' Dykes said. ''You poisoned the whole town
on your snake-oil liniment, and now you've got to explain how
come.''

*   *   *

Tom Sorrell had scarcely tasted food in three days. He had drunk too much whiskey and his stomach felt as tender as a rope burn. Now he was on milk and whiskey. One offset the other, but the milk stole some of the anger which was the product of the whiskey. *She's gone,* he would realize. *She's left me.* But then, *She'll come back when I go for her.* He believed that. He would finish Harlan, lock up his railroad and Dykes' coalfield like bonds in a strongbox, and take them to her as a present.

But as the whiskey ebbed in him he remembered Lovena's eyes when he punished her that night. For the first time he had known that she did not love him at all; that she never would love him. She regarded him the way any young girl regarded a man twice her age. It was easy to fool yourself that your money and your mature charms made up for the loose skin under your eyes and the eyebrows like badger hair. But when the whiskey burned low in him he knew she must have shuddered every time he touched her. Her father had put her up as collateral when Sorrell refused to help with the Magdalena Railroad, so she had come along.

So that was how she justified running off to Harlan. And now Harlan had somehow carried her up to the main line, and she was gone, and when the sign looked right he would try to follow her.

Sorrell was watching the plaza from his room over the bank. A while ago he had seen Clevis, Dykes, Chet Anders and some other ranchers assembling before the Gold Exchange Saloon. They were discussing the letter Sorrell had circulated. They all went into the saloon and shortly afterward Dykes came out and with his highstepping sand-crane gait hurried to Harlan's hotel. Sorrell buckled on his Colt and left the room. Harlan would rush to the saloon and count on his glib tongue to talk him out of the bind the letter had placed him in. Sorrell wanted to be there when he started excusing himself. He wanted to see the fury of the cattlemen boil over him like a mud-flow.

Crossing the plaza, he saw in his mind the catastrophe at the railroad bridge yesterday. It sent gooseflesh rippling over him. He had taken one look at the canyonful of splintered cars and bleeding cattle and ridden away. He remembered how Spurlock had looked after Harlan shot him. It suited Sorrell, except that in men's minds

Spurlock was allied to him. He had to handle that, as well as some other points in the Harlan mixup.

They would say: Sorrell set him up. He's as guilty as Harlan. Sorrell's arguments needed to be sound, but if they did not believe him it did not matter. Harlan had so much track to lay per month. After the ranchers ran him out his charter would go on the block for purchase by an approved bidder. Sorrell's connections were still good. He could get approval over any of these basin men, who were notched with one railroad failure already.

Sorrell walked to the saloon. He did not enter. He leaned against a post supporting the gallery. He could hear Anders' bull voice in the saloon overriding the voice of Day Clevis. Clevis was saying, "Well, I think we ought to let—" and Anders hit the bar and shouted, "A gut-shot rabbit's got more fight than you, Clevis!" and the rancher made some stiff response.

I wonder about that confession he was supposed to write me, Sorrell thought. He had not checked his mail since Lovena ran out on him.

Up the street he saw Harlan's dark head in the sidewalk traffic. He waited there and Harlan came in view with Dykes at his heels. Harlan's coat tails flapped. He looked at Sorrell without recognition. His features were deeply drawn with emotion. Then he recognized the rancher and halted. They were three feet apart and Jim Harlan's hand was on the slatted door.

"What's the matter?" Sorrell smiled. "Troubles?"

Harlan bunched his hand. Without warning he drove his fist into Sorrell's face like a pistol butt. The blow threw Sorrell sideways. He caught at the upright against which he was leaning. Then as the haze went out of his mind he felt Harlan's hand dragging him into the street and heard him shouting. Sorrell scarcely knew him. The man was wild. His mouth made a savage grimace as he smashed at Sorrell's face. The rancher took the blow on his forehead and dropped to his hands and knees, stunned. His strength and enormous anger saved him. Harlan pulled him up with both hands as men came clattering out of the Gold Exchange. Sorrell, on his knees, hooked an uppercut into Harlan's chin. Harlan reeled into the wall.

Sorrell went after him like a boar, then. He slammed a round-house left into Harlan's side and thundered a right into his head. He stamped on his foot with his bootheel. He drove to Harlan's jaw and Harlan stumbled into the crowd of men. Someone shoved him away. Sorrell measured as Harlan rushed in and threw a straight, murderous punch. But Harlan stopped short for the swing. His face was bloody and grim. Then a pair of arms went around him from behind and a man—Day Clevis—-jammed him up against the wall.

"Some of us may want a little of Harlan too, Sorrell! But he's going to talk first."

Sorrell tried to work around for another shot at Harlan, but several men came between them. He cooled, pulled out a blue bandanna and covered his bleeding mouth. Clevis let Harlan turn. Harlan's eyes were desperate. The beautiful green and red feathers of the fighting cock had become bedraggled, Sorrell reflected.

Anders stepped in with someone's copy of the letter in his fist and thumped Harlan's chest. "What about this letter? What've you got to say?"

Blood ran down Harlan's chin. "It's partly true," he said.

Anders raised both hands to quiet the men who began to talk. "So you're just a cheap medicine-show swindler with a little richer snake-oil to peddle, eh?"

"No, I was going to build a good railroad," Harlan said. "*Am,* I mean."

"Oh, no you weren't—ain't, I mean," Anders mocked. He smashed his fist with the big silver ring against his palm. "What did you figure to use for rails on this railroad—strap iron?"

Harlan looked at the growing crowd. "Listen, men—can I tell it? Can I tell you what I was doing?"

Day Clevis pulled out a gold pocket watch. "This had better be sixty seconds of the best talking you ever did. The rest of you understand this: I get first shot afterward. I lost three thousand dollars in that wreck!"

"You don't blame me for the wreck, do you?" Harlan demanded. "Didn't you see Spurlock's body on the cliff?"

Sorrell lowered his bandanna. "He was going to La Cinta on my orders, to look for Mrs. Sorrell. I don't think he had anything to do with the wreck. Why would he have?''

"Because he hated me," Jim said. "Or did you tell him to dump my train to teach me a lesson?"

"That would make sense," Anders scoffed. "After Sorrell'd set you up in business."

"Yes, he did," Harlan conceded. "But he found I wouldn't work his way. Tell them that," he suggested to the rancher. "Tell them the things that weren't in your letter."

Sorrell's bleeding mouth smiled. "Why don't I tell them where you learned your trade, mister? About your friend who died before a Mexican firing squad? He learned his way around a marked deck in Mexico, working with a cheapjack soldier of fortune. I doubt if any of their railroads ever carried freight."

Clevis asked sharply. "Then why did you make the arrangements for him to build this road?"

"Because I figured that with enough money, and me for a watchdog, he could build a good one. But he started bucking before he ever got started."

Clevis' eyes stayed on Sorrell's mouth.

"Why didn't Great Southern come in openly instead of sneaking in the back door?"

"You know why. Because they blocked your little one-horse road ten years ago. You'd have fought them every inch of the way. But the point was, the basin couldn't support a road then! There wasn't enough freight. And you proved you couldn't swing it financially, either. Railroad building isn't for amateurs. So," Sorrell shrugged, "I helped get Harlan started. He was Great Southern pick, not mine. Still I thought he wasn't a bad one," he admitted, "until he began talking about selling stock and getting the bank to float bonds for him."

"That's a lie," Harlan snapped. "I wouldn't even talk stock to Dykes."

Drawn with gloom, Dykes' face was long. "That's not quite true, Jim. You said you'd talk stock to me later."

"I was putting you off, Clancy. I never would have sold you any. Because the sale to Great Southern would have been for a token payment when it came, and you'd all have been cleaned."

Sorrell laughed. "Man, you're so stiff with ethics your back would break if you tried to bend over! Tell them about Mexico, Jim," he invited. "Tell them about the two hundred workmen who died on that Tehuantepec road!"

"They died of yellow fever," Harlan said, "along with a few villages who weren't working for us. You know what I'd rather tell them? About Tom Sorrell's disappearing railroad charter! This was really clever," he told the men. "His own lawyer wrote the charter! It's weaker than thin tea on a platter. He didn't tell me that until the other day. But ever since then he's been trying to force me to deal him in as a silent partner. All he wants is for me to bankrupt the road after I'm half finished, and let him take it over."

Sorrell regarded him steadily. "What would prevent someone else from taking over instead of me?"

Harlan frowned. "I don't know. But you said you could."

"You're scrambling," Sorrell smiled, "but not making much time, Jim."

Harlan glanced at the men around him. He looked tired and blocked. "Clancy—say—" he said. "Listen. It's a poor recommendation to admit that I was a swindler before I came here. But in Mexico it was different. At least it seemed different. We were swindling the government, and kicking back half the profits in bribes. But it wasn't any different, because in the long run it was people like you who did the paying. Only I had to come close to it before I could see that."

"No," Clevis told Harlan, "it ain't much of a recommendation." His hat was down over his face and his swarthy features were grim. Somehow that gotched-ear of his, which ordinarily seemed out of character for him, looked fitting. Sorrell sensed a core of wildness in him. "Didn't you know Great Southern would put the screws on us if they ever got into the basin? You were close enough to understand that, weren't you?"

"I'd never heard about you and Great Southern until I got here."

Chet Anders spat at Harlan's feet. "Hadn't, eh? You lying pig," he said. He threw Sorrell's crumpled letter in Harlan's face.

Harlan's shoulder moved back, but he held himself. "Clancy," he told Dykes earnestly, "I'm going to give you some advice. Think about it after you've cooled off. Get some financing and build this road yourself. I'll sell you the charter for ten dollars."

Old Dykes eyes squinted as if he were trying to read a newspaper at ten feet. "Where are we going to get that kind of financing?"

"Anywhere. With your coal claims and the freight prospectus you can work up, any bank will lend you the money to get started."

Dykes stroked his long nose, pondering. "You think we could?"

Sorrell saw the change starting in Clevis' face, too. And he knew the moment was now. As he stepped forward, he moved Dykes aside with his arm. He was face to face with Harlan.

"Now tell us why you killed Cam Travis. Had he caught on?"

Harlan swung at him. But Chet Anders caught his arm and butted him back into the broken plaster wall. "Hold him!" he shouted. Tom Sorrell reached Harlan and pinned his arms behind him. Over Harlan's shoulder Sorrell saw Anders' face—blunt, brutal, delighted. He saw Anders turn the jagged ring on his right hand so that the crude Aztec face carved in the silver was up.

Anders took his time, while Sorrell held Harlan. He set his weight, balanced, and then with his lips compressed threw an overhand blow into Harlan's face. On Harlan's cheekbone appeared a frosty pattern like the indentation of a snake's fangs, which immediately filled with blood and overflowed. Harlan stamped on Sorrell's arch and the rancher grunted and let him go. But Day Clevis and two other men, catching fire at last, piled onto him. they hauled him to a post, put his back to it, and locked his arms behind.

Chet Anders moved into position, one arm thrust forward, his fingers delicately spread, his other fist cocked, like a man heaving a stone. His face gleamed with animal enjoyment.

"Eight ball in the corner pocket!" he said. Then he drove into Harlan's face again. Sorrell grunted as he heard the meaty smack. He walked up as the Muleshoe foreman was measuring for another swing, and thrust him aside. He gazed into Harlan's eyes, half-smiling. They shared the memory, Sorrell thought, of that day in the wonderful private car called *Rio Arriba,* when Harlan had turned down his help and said, *All you ever need is jacks to open—and the guts to back them!*

Sorrell said to Anders, "I'm only holding jacks, Chet. Is that good enough to open?"

"He ain't apt to raise you!"

"Just one shot—that's all I want," Sorrell said.

The crashing explosion of his fist against Harlan's face was fine, but Harlan's reaction—the pure, distilled bitterness, the sink-your-teeth-in, bulldog stubbornness that gleamed in Harlan's eyes—somehow spoiled the effect of the blow.

By heaven, Sorrell thought, the fool never will get enough!

But for Harlan, the trouble was, they did not finish it. He wished he could pass out, but they left him drawling in a purgatory of misery. They took their shots at him and finally someone said to stop it, and he thought he heard a scuffle going on. Then a couple of men helped him to the hotel and left him sagging against the door for everyone to look at. His body ached from being kicked.

Was it that they didn't care to knock him out, or that they couldn't? He only knew that through it all he had held onto something in him as if he held a rope, and every time he swung out over the black waters he swung back on it. It seemed to be a determination to make himself understood. It was like getting yourself dirty and having to wash. God knew he had gotten hopelessly dirty, but the only way to feel clean was to be understood. And the only way to make himself understood. . . . What was he trying to do, anyway? He had forgotten.

He leaned for some time against the wall just inside the door of the hotel. Then he saw the entrance to the hotel bar and started for it. A man said, "Here, old fellow," and took his arm. But getting drunk would only lessen the pain, not the sickness. So he said, "No," and started an explanation of the problem, but before he got into it he found himself in the middle of the lobby. Then Joe Fowler came and led him to his room.

He was lying on the bed with his shirt off when Clarence Dykes came. It was early in the cold fall afternoon.

Jim heard him fussing around the room. Dykes did not speak to him and Jim had said all he had to say. After a while Dykes came to his bedside. His face was as long and glum as that of an old Indian.

"Your stuff's packed," he said. "I've got a rig waiting. You can drive to La Cinta and catch a train. Or I'll drive you."

"Thanks for your trouble. I can't go yet."

"You'd better, before somebody gets real hot and puts a bullet in you."

"It's not that. I'm just—" he spread one hand—"not going."

Dykes endeavored to seem tough, but his eyes gave him away. Dykes was a horned toad, spike-armored like a medieval charger, but inwardly shy and soft. Horrified by Jim's condition, he tried not to appear affected by it. Cut to the heart by having been tricked, he would not show his hurt.

"You better go," he said. "Know what's good for you."

Jim touched his face. "This hurts," he said. He put his palms on his sides. "Hurts like sin here, too." Then he put his hand over his heart. "But this is killing me."

"Don't break down," Dykes said. "All you lost was money. I lost—"

"You lost a dream. Clancy. That's the worst. That's why I can't go. I've got to build that railroad."

Tears came to Dykes' eyes. He squeezed them shut and began laughing silently. "Build it! *Build* it! No right-of-ways! No money. No faith. Jim, you kill me."

Jim struggled up on one elbow. "*You've* got money. I've got a charter. I'll give you the charter. You and the others finish it. But let me stay around to help. Let me beat off Sorrell when he tries to take over. You know he's going to."

"I know you say so."

Jim felt hemmed in by stone walls. He was in a prison he had helped construct. He shook his finger at Dykes. "All right, hear me, now. I'm going to finish it myself, if you won't. Great Southern's still back of me. I'll tell them how it goes with Sorrell. Think they won't back me? You don't know high finance. If I pay a thousand a month for specialists, they won't care whether they studied at M.I.T. or Colonel Colt's Trade School. Just so they get their road. But if I finish it for them, I'll have to give it to them."

"You won't finish it without right-of-ways."

Jim grinned. His mouth began to bleed again. "Man, I never even bothered with right-of-ways till I came here. I'll condemn every ranch in the valley. I'll knock heads together. But here's the point—I'm going to finish that road, and it will be a beauty."

Dykes went to stare into the alley, where autumn's cold breath was blowing leaves and rags of paper past the window. "Con-din-it," he sighed. "I wish we could have built it. Engines would have purred when they went over that road. All an engineer would have had to do was play pinochle with the train crew and watch the water level in the glass."

"Help me, Clancy." Jim's face twisted. "You need it as much as I do. You can bring them around for me. But I'm licked without you."

Dykes' bony head wagged. He walked to the door, turned the knob and gazed down at it. "They couldn't hear me if they were all wearing ear trumpets. This is a different town. It's bought its last bottle of snake-oil liniment. It's Sorrell's town and Chet Anders' town, now. Chet's smoking a big cigar and trying to buy land from Day Clevis for some kind of a crazy crossbreed cow he wants to raise on it. We'll never see the basin the way it was before you came and Cam Travis died."

The door closed. Jim lay back. The cold increased in the room and his thoughts went on like a screw into wood, blindly but taking a harder bite all the time. Suddenly he reared up and pulled the big ruby from his hand. He stared at it. Then he flung it into a corner. He lay back to stare at the ceiling with his open eye, and to think, and think . . .

Seated at one of Pearlie Owen's tables with Day Clevis, Anders plucked the cigar from his mouth with thumb and index and wiped the white ash into a saucer. "This is just an idea," he told the rancher. "But why don't you apply for some more forest range under the new grazing act? I think you could qualify. If you get it, you won't need your hay-ranch pasture."

"No." Clevis said. He was examining a torn knuckle on his right hand. His hat lay upside down on the table with his gloves in the crown.

Anders shifted farther onto the edge of the chair. "I ain't asking you to give the land away. I'll pay a sight more than it's worth. Come down to it though, it ain't worth so damn' much. Stonier than ten miles of graveyard."

"Don't fool with it, then. The best is none too good for you."

Anders felt the sting of Clevis' words. Patiently he spread his hands. "I'm taking over a run-down outfit and trying to make something of it," he said. "Ranch ain't house and fences, it's land and cattle. How can I improve the breed of cattle till I've got more land?"

Clevis glanced at him dryly. "Any time you want to get rid of those black Anguses, let me know."

Anders said quickly, "Will you swap pasture for cattle?"

Clevis said, "If Mrs. Travis and Hester are crazy enough to swap, I'm ready any time." Then he asked curiously, "What kind of a critter is it you're fixing to breed up, Chet?"

Anders explained in detail, quoting from copy books filled with ciphering, and family-tree charts he had constructed. Soberly, mouth pursed, Clevis nodded.

"Why don't you work a strain of camel in there somewhere and get a critter that won't need water?"

Anders' lips thinned. "I'll buy and sell you out twice before I'm through."

Clevis smiled and took his gloves out of his Stetson. Then the door opened behind them and the barred pattern of sunlight on the floor was broken by a silhouette. Anders turned his head. Crystals of ice formed in his belly. Sheriff Crowley stood there with a horsehide jacket over his arm. He seemed to send his gaze groping through the shadows. Then his eyes came to rest on Anders. Anders put the cigar back in his mouth. Crowley walked inside. The doors whipped closed. Crowley put a hand on Clevis' shoulder as he reached the table.

"Don't go, Day," he said. He looked like a very tired man. Lines surrounded his eyes like mud-cracks. He pushed his hat back and took a chair. He dropped the jacket on the table.

"Here's one for the book," he said.

"What's this?" asked Clevis, his hand turning the jacket. Then he said, "What the hell!" He had found the bloody sleeve. His gaze lifted slowly to the sheriff's face.

"It was near Lopez Canyon, where Cam died. Bill Holly and I were poking around—" Crowley stopped. "I want to ask you some questions, Chet," he said abruptly.

An unbearable excitement seemed to distend Anders' head, like dynamite hunting a seam. He wanted to scream. It's Sorrell's! The blood proves he killed Travis! But he puffed calmly on the twenty-five cent cigar, dispatched his hand to take it from his lips, and blow smoke at the harp lamp over the table.

"Why me?" he asked. "It ain't my coat."

"No, but you were in that area the day Cam was killed. Did you see anybody out there?"

"Not up close. Couple of punchers mending fence."

"See Tom Sorrell?"

Anders snapped a sharp glance at the sheriff. "Sorrell!" he exclaimed. "You don't reckon—"

"It's his jacket," Crowley said, staring intently at the foreman.

"How do you know?" Clevis asked.

"I recognize it. Rios, the bootmaker, made it for him."

Anders examined the stained sleeve and looked across the table at Day Clevis. "Sorrell!" he said. "A man like that—hell, it couldn't have been him," he declared.

"It could have been anybody," Crowley said. "But it happens to be Tom's coat."

Suddenly Day Clevis rose, overturning his chair. He stared furiously down at Chet. His face congested. "You and your bonehead ideas!"

Anders' shoulders sagged. "Where do I come into it?"

"If Sorrell killed Cam, then he was probably lying about Harlan, too! And the beating we gave him—"

"Harlan?" exclaimed Sheriff Crowley. "You beat Jim Harlan?"

Thumping the table slowly with his fist, Clevis told about it. "He ought to be in on this," he finished. "He's got a score to even.— *Blast you for a fool!*" he shouted at Anders.

"But he admitted—"

Clevis raised the table so that liquor, glasses and cigar ash spilled into Anders' lap. Then he shoved the table over on him. Anders fell back on the floor. He came onto all fours and scrambled up, his lips twisting back in a snarl. With both fists bunched he started for Clevis. But Crowley stepped forward.

"Cut that, Chet. Day, I'm surprised at you."

Clevis, staring at his fist, rubbed the reddened knuckles, frowning silently. "I'm going down and see Harlan, he growled.

"I'll go along. You too, Chet."

Anders' big shoulders moved in a shrug. "Why not? But I ain't making no manners to Mr. Harlan whatever you found."

They walked to the hotel. Chet was uneasy. He did not understand Crowley's manner. Did Crowley suspicion him? But facts were facts. In the lobby Clarence Dykes was standing at the front window gazing into the street, a lonely old man slapping his leg with a rolled newspaper. They walked to Harlan's room. Harlan let them in. When he saw Anders he stared with the most dogged fury Anders had ever seen in a man's face. But he did not stir. There he stood in pants and undershirt, his face swollen and cut so that no one would have recognized him. With his slitted eyes, he oddly resembled a cat.

Clevis walked forward. Harlan put up his hands in a fighting stance, but the rancher took his right hand and said, "God forgive us, Harlan. This ox-brained ramrod of Travis's—"

"Now, wait a minute!" Anders said.

"Shut up, both of you," Crowley snapped. "Harlan, do you know this jacket?" Harlan looked at the coat the sheriff held up, then shook his head. "You wouldn't of course. But it was worn by the man who killed Cam Travis. I found it in the brush early this morning, as I and Bill Holly were quartering for sign."

"Do you know whose it is?"

"It's Tom Sorrell's."

Harlan turned and pulled a gun and cartridge belt from the back of a chair. He buckled them on and then rousted through a clothespress for a shirt. A bloody shirt lay on the floor by the wash stand. A bubble of exaltation rose through Anders. The only dangerous thing had been Sorrell's glib tongue. But if it had no chance to wag. . . .

Crowley watched the railroad man. With raised brows he put his hands on his breast. "Does it seem more fitting that I, the law of this town, should talk to him first? Or shall we surround the building, burn it down, and kill him as he comes out?"

After a moment Harlan slumped on the bed. "You're right. I'm so—" He struck his chest. "So bottled up in here. Crazy. You don't know—I was sure he'd wrecked the train yesterday. And it made sense that he might even have killed Mr. Travis. But nobody would listen to me. Sheriff, when the time comes to take him, will you signal from the window? Let us in on it."

Crowley barely smiled. "I'll hang a lantern in the window if I need help." He went to the door. Anders watched Clevis squeeze Harlan's shoulder and stand there in remorse and embarrassment, shaking his head. At the door the sheriff turned back.

"Say, we found something else of Sorrell's out there, too. His wife."

"No fooling!" Harlan said.

"Sure enough. She's in a cabin on the old Shelton place. I wanted to give her safe conduct into town, but she said no, she was waiting for somebody. What she must have gone through with that bull!"

CHAPTER 18

SORRELL PEERED at himself in the mirror. It was cold in the rough upstairs bachelor room he called his camp. Shaving water was heating on the stove. He palmed the coffee-brown stubble on his jaws. His whiskers had taken on the oily smoothness of three-day stubble. You're a hell of a looking senator, he thought wryly. You look like a railroad detective.

He began stropping his razor. The operation was smooth and calming. He spat on the strop and wiped the blade back and forth with a silken whisper. The election is over, Senator, he reflected. Nothing to do now but count the ballots. Take plenty of time. Take a year or so to push Harlan officially out. He'll be gone by tomorrow, but give them time to forget him and his railroad. Then take it over. Give Dykes a little time, too. The fossilization of Clarence Dykes has been going on for years. Another year and he'll belong to archaeology, like a fish in a rock.

But the jagged end of something broken turned in Sorrell, Lovena, Lovena! He gazed down on the busy plaza, feeling the old empty hunger. If I could talk to her again . . . But Harlan had got her away, and she would never come back. He wished he could return to that night. He would lock her in her room this time and tell the servants she was not to leave the ranch. I would rather have her as a prisoner, he thought, than not at all. There was a species of satisfaction, at least, in having a woman by force, if you could not have her otherwise. Maybe that was the only workable man-and-woman relationship. If you treated them decently, they tried to make you over. When you slapped them around, they respected you as you were.

He poured water in the stoneware basin and began to work up lather in a mug. The downstairs door opened. Someone ascended slowly. Quickly he laid his hand on the walnut grip of his Colt. He set the shaving mug on the wash stand and placed himself near the table to wait. The man on the stairs mounted with a patient, heavy tread. Sorrell heard him pause outside the door.

"Tom? It's Crowley."

"Come in, come in!" Sorrell said heartily. Yet he wondered: *Why Crowley?* He took up the shaving things as the sheriff entered. "Sit down. A little late in the day for shaving, eh?"

Crowley glanced at him. "A little late in the week, you might say." He was carrying a coat of some kind, rolled inside out, which he laid across his knees as he sat down. A pulse throbbed in Sorrell's head. *He's found Anders' jacket!* He could not help staring at it.

"What've you got?" he asked.

"Jacket I'm taking Rios to mend. Say, Tom, I was out at the wreck yesterday with Bill Holly. He and I camped there last night and looked around some more this morning. I'll never forget it."

"I'm glad I wasn't there," Sorrell said.

Crowley frowned at him. "I was wondering how you'd explain Dick Spurlock being up there pouring it onto the survivors."

"I sent him there."

"You sent him!" Crowley repeated.

"I sent him to La Cinta. His orders were to quarter around the area on the way. Maybe that was his definition of quartering. It wouldn't be mine."

"What was he supposed to find?"

"Don't you know?" Sorrell asked quietly. "Don't they ever bring you the gossip?"

The sheriff's hand slowly rubbed the jacket. "You mean your wife? She's no concern of mine. But if Spurlock was looking for her, he must have lost his talent for tracking. He passed within a quarter-mile of her on the way."

Sorrell had been watching Crowley in the mirror. His hand came down with the shaving brush. He was incapable of hiding what he felt. He turned. "The fort!" he explained. "She was there, then, that night—"

"I don't follow you."

Sorrell's face had a hard shine. "A couple of nights ago. She'd packed and taken off. Every young wife has to do it at least once." His mind was far ahead, running, sprawling, running again, wild with a dark joy; but he had to keep his mouth going with the things Crowley expected.

"I rode out looking for her and ran into Hester Travis, at the fort. She was waiting for Anders to come by. He'd gone back to town for something. She swore she hadn't seen Lovena. But I see now. She was hiding her."

I'll find her. I'll cut her off if she heads for La Cinta!

"Is she still there?" he asked. "When was this—last night?"

"This morning, as we were riding in. No, she's not at the fort. She's—never mind," Crowley said, "that's not why I came."

"Where is she?" Sorrell thumped the mug down and began wiping his hands on his trousers. Like a hound, his mind cornered the answer. The Shelton place! Within a quarter-mile of the road, Crowley had said. So that was what had ailed Dick Spurlock! That's why he had come up looking like death warmed over. He had found her and knew she was waiting for Harlan. And Spurlock must have been gone on her too. . . .

Sorrell wanted to shout, *Get out of here! I've got things to do!* But Crowley was rubbing the rolled coat and frowning.

"What was Spurlock's idea?" he asked. "He must have had some motive in wrecking the train."

"Sheriff," Sorrell said levelly, "I've heard of train wrecks happening by themselves. Those rails hadn't been used in ten years."

"But they were sound, except where Spurlock had pried two of them loose. Two men did it. I found their bootprints all over the grade. Were you the other man?"

Sorrell's face hardened. "I'll fight a railroad in the senate, but not that way."

"Spurlock was your man."

Sorrell closed one fist, and opened it. "Will you keep this quiet?"

"If I can."

"Dick Spurlock was in love with Lovena. So is Harlan. I realize how that makes me look, but that's the way it is. Dick thought she was running away with Harlan, whereas she was just running away from me. I suppose he was trying to get even with Harlan.''

Crowley passed his hand over his bald head. He nodded. "That follows. Now tell me one more thing: Why did you kill Cam Travis?''

Sorrell did not move. He saw that the sheriff had drawn his gun. With his free hand, Crowley shook out the coat he had said he was taking to be mended. Sorrell recognized it. The sleeve was caked with dark stains. "That's mine," he said blankly.

"Thanks. I'll write that into the record: Prisoner admits it was his. You weren't thinking fast. A half-mile away ain't far enough to ditch a thing like this.''

A dark flood washed into Sorrell's mind. He walked toward Crowley. A chair was in the way and he knocked it aside.

"Sheriff, will you use whatever brains you were born with? Would a man commit murder and leave his name and address by the body?''

"How long would he dare carry a bloody coat around with him? He'd have to ditch it quick.''

Sorrell took the sheriff by the shoulders and shook him violently, ignoring the gun in his belly.

"Will you use your brains? Will you tell me why I wouldn't at least have buried the damned thing?''

"Scared men do strange things.''

Sorrell felt his Colt sliding from the holster as Crowley took it. He backed off a step. "Earn your pay, Crowley. *Think!* I was in town. I couldn't have killed him.''

"How do I know that?''

Now the rancher's arms hung straight and he wagged his head. "I have been an ass, Sheriff. I have been the most unmitigated ass who ever lived. I know who killed Travis. I came along just after it happened. I saw him ride away.''

Crowley smiled. "I'll bet it was Spurlock again. He was going to get rid of you and marry your wife.''

"It was Chet Anders. I was coming back from La Cinta. I watched Anders—that is, I was almost certain it was him—cut the horse's throat to put it out of its misery. But I didn't want to accuse him until I was sure. I wrote down everything I saw and put a copy in the safe at the bank and mailed myself the other copy. It's in my box at the post-office.''

Crowley was standing, now, his face as stubborn as the two Colts he held. ''Yes, I wondered about Chet's new jacket. But I also wonder about this: Couldn't you both have been involved? Otherwise why would you have been afraid to come to me, tell me your suspicions and let me do the investigating?'' He shook his head. ''Come on, Tom,'' he said. ''This is too complicated for a simple-minded man like me. I'm going to turn it over to the county prosecutor.''

Sorrell put his hand on the back of a chair. He wanted to pick it up and smash it over Crowley's head, but he couldn't.

''Let's go,'' Crowley said. ''I'll bring your things to the jail later.''

If a thing could be criminally ridiculous, Sorrell thought, this situation qualified. Lawyers could make his case solid as iron; but Divide was a geyser with a thin crust of mud over it. Resentment over Travis' death, and the wrecking of Harlan's train could break the crust. The case would never go to trial in this town, not while there was six feet of rope for sale. And while he sat in jail wondering when they would find the guts to lynch him, Harlan would go sporting off with Lovena.

Crowley's eyes were sleek with satisfaction. Little men, little towns—they took revenge seriously. I'll get justice, Sorrell thought, but not in Divide, New Mexico. If I get it, it will be a long way from here.

''As a special favor,'' he said, ''will you let me wire a lawyer? There aren't enough legal brains in this town to put two halves of a cracked saucer together.''

He opened the door and felt Crowley come up behind him. ''All the lawyers in the Territory,'' the sheriff said.

''What happens to Anders? I suppose he sits in the jury box?''

''I'll get to Anders. Right now he's on his way to Muleshoe—or so he said. He said Hester was expecting him. Maybe he was just shy about facing you.''

Understandable, Sorrell thought. But Anders was a smudge which he could wipe off at leisure. Sorrell's mind kept veering toward the Shelton cabin, obsessed by the encounter with Lovena.

"Let's go," Sheriff Crowley prodded.

Sorrell walked onto the landing. Without warning, he retreated one stride and collided with the sheriff. His hand snapped back and caught Crowley's wrists. Crowley shouted. One of the guns exploded into the floor. The roar buffeted Sorrell's eardrums. He pulled Crowley's arms forward, pivoted on the landing so that their backs were to the stairs, and lunged back against the sheriff. Crowley lost his footing as the other gun went off and smoke rose about them.

Sorrell turned just as Crowley crashed full length on the stairs. Crowley's features twisted with expected pain, then his face went slack. Sorrell saw his head bounce. He plunged after the sheriff, tore the guns from his hands and raised one like a hatchet. But Crowley was limp. Sorrell dropped the sheriff's gun and holstered his own.

His thinking was cold and clear.

To get away. To find Lovena. To get money and leave the Territory. In the East he could raise money, and they would have to extradite him. But he realized he would have to go by the ranch to get money from his strongbox, and to pick up the kind of horses he would need. Then he would cut north a few miles to the Shelton place, get Lovena, and bear east into the mountains.

Slowly he descended the stairs. Crowley must have talked to someone before he came up, so they would be watching the door. They must have heard the shots. He kicked the door open and pressed against the wall. He could see a dazzling wedge of the bare ground, some leafless poplars, and a number of men stiff as stone soldiers in a park, staring at the bank buildings. Two men were running across the ground from the other side of the square.

He raised the Colt and fired at the man in the lead, who was Jim Harlan, and saw him stumble and fall on the ground. But he knew he had not hit Harlan because he heard the bright tinkle of glass from a window in the hotel. Harlan squirmed and Sorrell saw a glint of metal in his hand. He saw a scurry of dust on the ground. The bullet penetrated the open door and crashed through the stairs. There was the loud report of it. Sorrell raised his Colt again.

CHAPTER 19

Jim AND the others had walked to the hotel lobby with Crowley, but the sheriff would not let them go any farther. "If Sorrell sees you roosting in front of the hotel like a row of buzzards," Crowley said, "he won't be there when I go up. Stay inside."

"No sir," Chet Anders protested. "Miss Hester's counting on me being back before dark. I'm taking off."

"What's the matter?" Crowley scoffed. "No curiosity? Don't you want to see what Tom Sorrell looks like in a jail cell?"

Anders showed them a sour grin. "I've seen what they all look like in jail cells—cowboys, bankers, railroad promoters. He'll spend the rest of his life till they hang him singing sad songs about being framed."

He walked outside. Crowley, standing in the doorway, peered across the plaza at the blocky bank building on the far corner. Without a word he left the hotel. Jim watched him cross the walk, speak to a man who spoke to him, and stroll across the square. The autumn sun was in Crowley's face. Jim heard a man come up beside him and Day Clevis.

"Where's Crowley going?" Mr. Dykes asked.

"To arrest Tom Sorrell," Clevis said. "It seems we were wrong about Jim."

Jim turned. "Just part wrong."

"Part wrong, part right. Like lots of people."

"Sorrell!" Mr. Dykes exclaimed. "What's he going to arrest him for?"

"Murder," Clevis said. "Tom Sorrell killed Cam. At least they found his jacket over there. Crowley's gone to work him over."

Dykes nodded slowly as he stared at the bank building. "Yes, I can believe it. I can believe that a man who'd murder a railroad in cold blood would murder a man."

"It hasn't been murdered," Jim said quickly. "If you bury it, Clancy, you bury it alive. I told you how you could save it."

The three of them stood in a small preserve of silence in the busy lobby. "Would Great Southern have to be in it?" Day Clevis asked.

"If you give the word, I'll pull the rug from under them tomorrow. I'll turn my charter over to you. All you'll need then is financing."

"Where do you come into it?" Clevis asked.

"I don't. I'm out of it."

"Do you want to be out of it? I mean, you've built railroads before, and whatever we do, we'll need a strawboss."

It seemed to Jim that Dykes looked pleased at what Clevis had said. "If it suits you to keep me on," Jim said humbly, "I'd sure like to build one railroad that I wouldn't be afraid to ride on."

Clevis scratched his gotch-ear. "It just seems to me that a cow country without a railroad is going to be froze out by the Midwest stockmen before long. We're a long way from our markets."

"Whatever you may decide to do about Jim Harlan," Jim said, "I think I know what Cam Travis would have said about the railroad—get your financing and build it!"

Color stirred under Mr. Dykes' thin skin. His eyes glittered. "Really think we could get financing?"

"If I get the financing lined up, will you build it?"

Dykes looked at Day Clevis. "Will we go broke?" Celvis asked.

"You couldn't go broke if you tried. You'll reach Dykes' coal fields in fifteen miles. After that you'll have a pay load and Dykes will be making more money than any of us ever saw before."

Dykes' chest swelled. Suddenly he reached in his pocket and pulled out a gold eagle. "There's ten dollars," he said, handing it to Jim. "We're buying your charter. What do you say, Day?"

Clevis hesitated. "After what happened to my cattle, I'm probably crazy. But I'll take chips in your game."

Jim shook hands with them. "I'll get the paper right now. Joe Fowler can witness the transfer of title." He did not want them to sleep on it and grow cautious. But as he started from the window, he heard a flat, explosive sound. He halted. They looked at one another. Then they hurried onto the porch of the hotel. Jim heard a man on the walk ask another:

"Wasn't that a shot?"

Jim began running across the plaza. Some teamsters repairing harness under a tree stared at him as he passed. Halfway across the square, he saw the door to Sorrell's outside stairway fly open. He drew his Colt as he ran. Then he saw a flash inside the staircase and a bullet snapped past him. He reached toward the ground and hit it running. It knocked the wind out of him. He lay hunched against the earth. He heard glass break far behind him. He heard the hard pulse of the gunshot from the bank. Jim thrust his Cold before him and took a bead on the open doorway. It was a blank rectangle of shadow. He fired, and dust whipped before him. He could hear wood splinter in the stairway.

Another shot burst from the opening and the slug hurled grit in Jim's face. He saw Tom Sorrell dart from the stairway, cut back along the sheet-metal tunnel and duck beneath it. He wondered about Crowley. He cocked the gun and waited to see Sorrell duck into sight to take a shot at his pursuers. When Sorrell did not appear again, he knew he had reached the alley behind the bank. Jim got up and ran on. He heard horses moving as he reached the bank. He reached the stairway and moved along close to the wall. But after a moment he heard the horses running. He ran hard down the pebbly wall. He came into the alley and saw Tom Sorrell, mounted on a bay and leading a second saddle horse, swerving into a side street at the far end of the alley.

Jim rested his gun on his forearm to take his shot. He was breathing hard. The gun wavered. He fired. The bullet struck Sorrell's saddle and he saw white splinters break from the saddle-swell. Sorrell's squarish body turned and sunlight sparkled on his Colt. He fired twice at Jim. Then he bent over the horn and took the horses down a lane of small adobe houses toward the river road.

There was a small stable behind the bank where Sorrell evidently had kept his mount. He meant to make the chase a fast one. He had taken his own horse and a second for a change when it gave out.

Jim took a horse from a stall and tightened the cinch. The stirrups were very short. Mounted, he rode with his knees drawn up like a jockey's. The horse had an unnatural mincing gait which would wear it out fast and cover no ground at all. Jim quirted it with his hand. When he reached the river road, he could see Sorrell's dust far ahead. Mexicans, chickens, and oxcarts had pulled out of the cottonwood-sheltered road to let him pass. Jim kept riding.

After a mile he gave up. He was riding back when Day Clevis and three men caught up with him. "He's riding and leading," he told them. "You'd better pick up extra mounts. Seen Crowley yet?"

"No," Clevis said grimly, "But we'll see Sorrell before we quit."

Watching them lope down the road, Jim did not feel so sure of it as they did. Sorrell was riding a good horse and had a change of mounts. Lack of speed would not be what gave him to the posse.

When Jim reached the bank again, they had carried Sheriff Crowley out and laid him on the boardwalk with his hat under his head. Doctor Watkins was already there, coatless and bare-headed. Jim stood in the crowd of men looking down at the lawman. "Is he shot?" he asked Watkins.

"Just slugged. But slugged good."

Crowley opened his eyes and saw Jim in the group. "Where's Sorrell?" the sheriff asked.

"He took off," Jim said. "But they'll drag him down. Here or in some tank town. Don't worry about him."

Crowley groaned. "It was my fault. I should have watched him closer. I'd baited him till he was half crazy. I told him we'd found his wife. Then when I let him know he was going to jail, he went crazy."

Suddenly Jim felt as though he had been knifed in the bowels. "Did you tell him where Lovena is?"

Crowley hesitated. "No. He don't know where she is."

"I hope he doesn't figure it out," Jim said.

Crowley looked around him. "Boys, I think something official ought to be done about catching him. Somebody will have to send wires to La Cinta and El Paso for me. Find my deputy and get a posse started. And listen!" he added. "You're looking for Chet Anders, too. Sorrell gave me a tall story about seeing Anders kill

Travis. I figure it's about half true, I reckon they were in it together."

"Anders!" Jim exclaimed. "Why would he kill Travis?"

"Why would Sorrell? They both hated Cam. And Cam had just fired Chet. But it was Sorrell's coat I found in the brush. Mind me, now. I want them both, dead or alive."

For a time Jim considered going with the posse. But he was less optimistic than the possemen. It would be a long hunt through the hills. In his present condition he might not last it out. He watched them ride out half an hour later. Clarence Dykes stayed with him. He walked to the barber shop with Jim and had a haircut while Jim had the swellings under his eyes leeched. Jim reclined with his boots on a red-plush stool. Dykes talked railroad, but Jim did not listen. He gazed up at the pattern stamped into the tin ceiling. It resembled a maze to befuddle rats. Up and down a maze in his mind Jim was pursued by a sharp-nosed worry. Crowley said he had not told Sorrell where Lovena was. But Sorrell might figure it out.

The door opened and a rush of cold air swirled in.

A Mexican boy said in Spanish, "I carry a letter for James Harlan. The man at the hotel say he is here."

Jim extended his hand. "I'm Harlan." He took the letter and gave the boy a tip. Lying there, he tore it open. It was in Hester's writing.

> *Jim: I'm worried about Mrs. Sorrell, now that we have the news about Tom Sorrell. Bill Holly and I are driving over to bring her to the ranch. Since she is a sort of project of yours, will you come over as soon as possible and tell me what to do with her? Also, may I have my hair back some day? I could use it for a switch.*

Jim reared up in the chair. "That's fine," he said. "Let the rest go."

"I can bring that lip down," the barber insisted. "I sent for a piece of ice."

"Let it go." Jim groped into his coat. "Clancy, I'm going out to Muleshoe." He left hurriedly. He had a foolish urge to run to the stable. So Hester was in it, now—bringing Lovena from cover into the open, where Sorrell, if he had not already decoded Crowley's secret, might see them both in the buggy!

He bought a pint of whiskey in the hotel bar, drank some of it, and hurried to the stable.

Sorrell was not simple. He was crazy where Lovena was concerned, but craziness and craft had the same sharp eyes. Sorrell might head for the ranch, get money and horses, and head north with his eyes open. Mounted on Cameron Travis' rosewood bay, Jim left Divide on the county road.

CHAPTER 20

IN THE ranch house kitchen Hester and her aunt sat up late the night after Harlan's train was wrecked. A puncher of Clevis's who had been with the train had ridden in with the news that afternoon. Chet, Bill Holly and some other men drove wagons out to help move the injured to town. Night came and one of the cowboys returned.

"Pretty fierce," he grunted. "Chet's drivin' a wagon to Divide. Crowley asked Bill to help cut sign or whoever done it."

"Then it wasn't an accident?"

"Nope," the puncher said.

Oh, good heavens! Hester thought. Is it possible he'll think I did it?

"Is Jim Harlan hurt?" she asked.

"Not bad."

She closed her eyes and thanked God. She and Aunt Carrie waited up late, drinking coffee. Most of the time since Uncle Cam died, Hester's aunt had sat in the parlor with her hands folded, gazing out the window. Her weeping showed only when she touched the corners of her eyes with a handkerchief. She had Hester listen to some of the poems he had written her.

But now, nearing midnight, Hester had to tell her something. "Did you know I was away last night?"

"Where, dear?"

"Chet and I and some of the men rode over and burned Harlan's private car."

Carrie Travis removed her spectacles and peered at her. "That isn't true!"

"I told him I would, you know. And after he proved he was dishonest by failing to get Tom Sorrell's signature and refusing to take our yearlings, I decided it was time to do it." Hester's lips curved slightly. "Do you know how he paid me back?"

Her eyes shone as she unpinned her hair. A large swatch was missing on the right side.

Her aunt gasped. "Why, child, you're a sight!"

"He would have cut it all off, accept that just then he discovered he was in love with me."

"How can you say he loves you when he means to elope with that Sorrell woman? Have nothing to do with a triflin' man, Hester!" Aunt Carrie hesitated. "Do you mean he *told* you he loved you?"

"No, but I know it." She slipped into a revery. On the shelf a clock resolutely tapped out the seconds. "He loves me, but he wouldn't say it, because he's dishonest."

"How can you tell all that while a man's cutting off your hair?"

"Well, in the first place he stopped cutting and kissed me—hard—so he probably loves me. In the second place he was going to tell me so, but decided against it. So he's dishonest, and doesn't want to be slowed down by a love affair when it comes time to leave the basin with a suitcase full of money."

Her aunt shook her head in confusion and went upstairs to bed.

Shortly after noon the next day, Bill Holly returned to the ranch, crusty and unshaven. When he tapped at the kitchen door, Hester went into the yard with him. The range foreman was restless. With his thumbnail he picked at the unplastered adobe wall, gouging out bits of straw.

"Well, that train was right shook up," he said.

She questioned him about it. With his moist, bulging eyes roving, he answered abstractedly.

"Miss Hester," he said finally. "Miss Hester—"

"Well, what, Bill?"

"Sheriff Crowley say anything to you about your uncle?"

"Just the nice things you'd expect him to say, that's all."

"But nothing about him being killed by somebody?"

All along there had lain in her mind a suspicion like a small, dirty coin that she did not care to pick up. But now it was being placed in her hand. She turned to close the kitchen door.

"Bill," she said, "what is it?"

With her back to the building, her gaze on a small compact cloud in the sky, she listened to him. Tears filled her eyes. When he related the finding of Tom Sorrell's jacket in the brush, she became alert again.

"But he wouldn't! I don't think he considered Uncle Cam important enough to kill."

"I don't know. I reckon Crowley will find out. It was his jacket, that's for sure. Something else he lost out there, too—Missus Sorrell. We found her."

If Holly had not reminded her of it, she might have forgotten Mrs. Sorrell, waiting in the cabin while all this was going on. She said, "Thank you, Bill. We won't say anything for a while."

Sitting alone in her room, it was like trying to listen to several conversations at once. But one voice became prominent. She went to the window to gaze toward the hills shaping the basin on the west, where Lovena Sorrell was hiding. She hoped Sheriff Crowley didn't say anything to Sorrell about finding his wife, because if Sorrell broke out of jail . . . if he found her . . .

She turned to go downstairs. She must bring Lovena to the ranch, where she could stay until she was ready to leave. If he would murder a man, he would kill an unfaithful wife. But pride halted her hand before she opened the door. "Have I been flirting with someone you're trying to catch?" Mrs. Sorrell had mocked her.

Hester did some needlework. After she pricked her finger twice she threw the hoops on the bed and snatched a hooded cape from the armoire. She snugged the cord about her neck and ran downstairs to find Bill Holly. He was carrying wood to a fire boiling under a cauldron in the yard, where a Mexican woman was making soap.

"Bill, we're going after Mrs. Sorrell," she said.

Holly dropped the wood and brushed his hands. "Now, I was thinking that myself," he said. "Two good reasons not to worry—Sorrell's going to jail and Crowley ain't talkative anyhow. But we can be over there and back in four-five hours, and then nobody will need to think about it any more."

"Exactly," Hester agreed. "Hitch a buggy while I write a note to Mr. Harlan. I think he ought to know what's going on out here."

She wrote the note to Harlan and instructed a Mexican boy to take the fastest horse in the corral and carry the note to Divide. Yet as she and Holly drove out, she could not put her mind at ease.

A short distance from the ranch they encountered Chet Anders riding in. Uneasiness brooded in Anders' rough-cut features.

"What's the word?" Holly asked him.

"No news," the foreman said. "I didn't bother to hang around after Crowley came in."

"Haven't you any curiosity at all?" Hester exclaimed. She was provoked because Chet might have brought important news from town, and hadn't.

"I didn't want to see it," Anders said. "I ain't much of a hand for lynchings."

"They aren't talking about lynching him, surely!" Hester exclaimed.

"Well, some of them—"

"But you say they hadn't arrested him yet?"

"Crowley told us about it in the saloon. Then we went to Harlan's room and told him."

Hester's eyes roved his face. "Why Harlan?"

"Clevis' idea. We'd cleaned his plow this morning. There was this letter from Sorrell—" Anders recounted it disconnectedly, shrugging it all off as a fight where there was little choice between the contestants, and he took no interest in how he resulted. "I still say he had it coming."

"How did he seem?" Hester asked.

Chet's grin used only half his mouth. "Beat up. Has a hare-brained idea that Dykes and the others can raise money to finish the railroad and he'll sell them the charter. Of course he lays it all at Sorrell's door, now. Know what I think? Harlan will sink the money he gets out of the charter in brass jewelry, and sell it for thousand dollars."

Hester bit her lip, her fingers tightly linked. "No, Chet. That isn't it. Give the man credit. He's had a change of heart."

"How does that work, Miss Hester, when a fella don't have no heart?"

Hester spoke briskly. "Well, if you don't know whether Tom Sorrell's in jail, we'll have to go on with what we were about to do.

Bill and I are going after Mrs. Sorrell. We think she'd be safer with us. You come along,'' she added.

The foreman opened his mouth as if to argue. Then he shrugged and fell in beside the surrey. Yet he seemed glum, she thought, like a man riding in a cotton shirt who has just sighted a blue norther bearing swiftly across the prairie.

Cameron Travis' horse was a fine traveler. It moved with a high, steady singlefoot that ate up the road and did not tire the rider nor the horse. As Jim rode toward Fort Quanah, he took the silken coil of Hester's hair from his pocket. He pressed it against his cheek. He could smell perfume in it. Very subtle it was, unlike Hester when she had a quirt in her hand. Jim laughed to himself. He never had fooled her. Well, she had the laugh on him, now. That night, she had been in love with him, as much in love as he was. But what about now, when she knew everything about him?

Jim felt sick, realizing that she knew all the things that were wrong with him, but none of the things that were right. He wanted to explain it all. But where and how could he start?

He passed Fort Quanah with a little tug of emotion. Every acre of this basin seemed to be scented with memories of Hester. He took a moment to scan the range across Iron Creek. Sorrell's headquarters buildings were miles away. He could not see them. He saw no horsemen, either.

The road forked here. The left fork mounted steeply into the foothills and on up to La Cinta. The right fork wound across the range, forded the creek, and went on to Travis' Muleshoe ranch. He rode a short distance up the La Cinta road toward the Shelton cabin and saw a buggy and horseman leaving the orchard. He rose quickly in the saddle. It could not be Sorrell, for he would not be traveling in a buggy. But who was the rider?

Then he realized Hester must have driven over to take Lovena home with her. Maybe the rider was Bill Holly. He felt relieved.

But before riding on, he threw a precautionary glance behind him. He could still see the buildings of the fort, the old adobe walls ruddy in the late sunlight. The sun washed the surface of the creek. Suddenly Jim squinted. He shaded his hand. Two riders were fording the stream. No, only one rider, but he was leading a saddle horse. Sorrell!

Jim pulled Fowler's carbine from under the stirrup. He wheeled the pony, shocked and indecisive. If he tried to block Sorrell, and Sorrell dropped him or swung wide around him, the rancher would ride straight on and catch the buggy. Hester was in it as well as Lovena. No, they ought to be warned.

He looked with quick hope beyond Sorrell, across Iron Creek, over the blunted hills of the basin. But Sorrell's pursuers were not in sight.

Jim rode down the slope, waving the gun. The buggy kept on going. He saw the rider turn a moment later when he shouted. The man wheeled his pony and the metal of a gun flashed in the sunlight. Jim shouted, "It's Harlan! Wait up!"

When he reached them, he saw that the rider was Chet Anders. Bill Holly was driving the buggy with Hester beside him. Lovena sat stiffly on the rear seat of the surrey. Hester put out her hand to Jim. She was smiling. Jim jarred Anders out of the way as he went to the buggy. He caught Hester's hand. She reached up to touch his battered face.

"Poor Jim! It was a hard way to make easy money, wasn't it?"

He gazed earnestly into her eyes, wanting to make her understand. "It wasn't really the money, Hester. Some day maybe I can tell you." He turned to Holly. "Ever drive a sulky?"

Holly looked him over. "Never had time to learn."

"You've got time now. Head for the ranch, and drive that thing as though you were in a race. Company's coming."

Anders seized his arm roughly. "What company?" A bright grain of fear lay in his eyes. "Are you talking about Sorrell?"

"Yes." Jim glanced at the dark-haired girl in the back of the rig. "Lovena," he said. "I'm sorry it worked out like this. But Bill will get you to the ranch. Chet and I will hold him off here."

"You're going to leave me alone, with Tom coming?" Lovena demanded. Her hands were clenched in her lap.

"Holly will be with you. This is the only way. Chet," he said, "you and I will try to head him off. He might swing around one of us, but he can't get by both."

"I stay with the wagon," Anders stated. "I ain't leaving the women to that ox."

"You're going with me," Jim said. "If that ox gets in firing range of the women, then we'll have a real worry."

"Do as Jim says, Chet," Hester ordered.

"Chet," Lovena said, "I'd feel better if you stayed."

Hester turned angrily. But Chet looked into her tense but smiling face and winked. "You see how it is," he said to Jim. "The lady says stay with the wagon. Bill, shake up the lines."

Lovena tilted her face triumphantly to Jim. Jim turned and caught Anders by the front of his jacket. He drew his Colt.

"If I'm not going to have the use of you, I'd as soon leave you right here. You go with me or you don't go anywhere." It was not a good time, he decided, to tell him that he was going to jail, anyway.

Anders' jaw muscles ridged. Through his tawny eyes Jim could see the canny measuring of his brain.

"Sure, Mr. Harlan. You're the doctor."

"As long as I've got your hardware, I'm the doctor." Jim took his Colt and secured it under his belt. He kept his own gun in Anders' stomach and drew the foreman's saddle-gun. "Now ride up to the road and I'll be right behind you. You'll get your guns when you need them."

The wagon moved away. Anders started up the long slope to the road. Jim followed. He reckoned Sorrell would be past the Muleshoe fork and coming up the La Cinta road. He looked back to wave at Hester. She had turned up the hood of her cape. She waved, but her face was pale under the dark hood.

Jim caught up with Anders. They started down the easy fall of the road. There was an edge to the wind which hissed through the brush. It made his eyes water as he searched for Sorrell. He saw him almost at once—riding at a jog-trot toward the Muleshoe fork of the road, his dust whipping away on the wind. The rancher's arm was extended as he brought the spare horse along. Jim touched Anders' arm.

"There he is!"

They watched him rein in at the fork and gaze east. Then his head turned and he was looking up the short swing of road to where Jim and the foreman waited. Jim could hear Anders' breathing. Sorrell

was less than half a mile away, staring at them as they watched him.
Suddenly he dropped the lead rope of the second horse and spurred
him away on an oblique line to their right, up the slope of the
foothills.

"Here we go!" Jim said. He gave Anders his guns. Anders
holstered the Colt and carried the carbine. They loped out on a line
which would intercept Sorrell if he tried to pass them on the right.
They rode hard for a few moments and then Sorrell wheeled the
horse to cut back in the other direction. But he held the pony an
instant, and Jim said breathlessly:

"We split up. Head him off if he tries it again. I'll hold him down
here. If he tries to go between us, we'll close in."

Anders studied the rancher. Sorrell's pony moved restlessly. You
could not tell which way he meant to ride. You only knew he would
move soon and quickly.

"This is no good," Chet argued. "If he comes between us we'll
be shooting at each other."

"We'll drop him before that. If he makes a run, dismount and
make your shots count."

"I've got an idea," Anders said narrowly. "Me and Sorrell had a
little deal about his wife. If I spotted her I was to help him get her. So
he may figure I'm still sort of on his side." He paused. "Do you
want to take him alive?"

"I don't care."

"Alive would be better, and no risk to you. I'll ride toward him
with my hands up. If he don't let me come in close, I'll have my Colt
in my lap and give it to him. If he does let me come up, I'll give him
some cock-and-bull story and then tag him behind the ear."

Jim looked at him. "That sounds like one of your tricks, all
right."

"I get results, don't I?" Anders grinned.

Jim watched Sorrell ride slowly on the same line he had taken
before, very straight in the saddle, a heavy-shouldered man in a gray
coat with his Stetson on the side of his head. In a moment Sorrell
would be riding hell-for-leather in one direction or another. If they
tried to drop him from here the range would be too far, and while
they were riding closer they could not fire accurately. One of them
might stumble and then Sorrell would be loose.

"Go ahead," he said. "But it had better not be a trick on the wrong man. I'll have your whole back to shoot at."

"*Sorrell!*" Anders shouted. He raised his right arm and jogged away. His left hand, in his lap, held reins and Colt. Sorrell did not stir as the foreman came on. Jim estimated the range at about four hundred yards. He looked down at Joe Fowler's gun. The sights were not for sniping. The gun was a large caliber repeater with dirt and lint in every crevice. Jim opened the breech and the copper jacket of the shell he ejected was crusty with verdigris. He reamed the chamber with his finger, ejected all the shells and replaced them with cartridges from his belt.

Anders rode easily over the bare tilt of range. Jim heard him shout again but could not distinguish his words. Sorrell made no motion. Anders was two hundred yards from Jim when he suddenly quirted his horse with the reins. Lying along the neck of the pony, he headed at a hard run for a brushy notch in the foothills. Jim was shocked. He could not believe even Anders' code would sanction this kind of treachery. He threw his gun to his shoulder, but then he thought: Save your shells. Watch Sorrell. He's one jump from kings' row now.

He saw Sorrell raise his saddle-gun and follow Anders in his sights. Sorrell took plenty of time, and while he aimed Jim began riding toward him. He saw the rancher rock slightly with the recoil of the gun. The powder smoke was torn from the rifle muzzle by the breeze. Jim saw Anders straighten and drop his revolver. He watched Anders sag. The foreman fell sidewise into the brush. His foot remained caught in the stirrup. The pony began kicking at him. Jim ran his eye over the range and realized the kind of a shot Sorrell had made.

Sorrell's body pivoted and he cocked the gun and took aim on Jim. Jim flinched and swerved the horse aside. Sorrell snapped a quick shot which tore the air a few feet from Jim. Jim reined to a stop and raised his rifle. He fired, but the bullet landed far short. The gun was worthless at over a hundred yards. Sorrell was patiently lining his sights. The sun was in Jim's face, silhouetting the rancher.

Jim dismounted quickly. He knelt and raised the carbine. Sorrell let the shot go. Instantly he spurred away to Jim's left. The bullet struck the ground and whined between Jim and the horse. The horse began to pitch away into the brush. Jim ran after it. He had to dive on the trailing reins to catch the horse. He got up skinned and frightened, and out of the corner of his eye saw Sorrell moving widely toward the river. He would cut back in a moment and be between Jim and the buggy.

Jim mounted on the run and loped downhill. He fired as he rode. Dust puffed ten yards behind Sorrell. He fired again and the bullet dropped short. *I can't stop him with this cannon,* he thought hopelessly. Poor gun, fine horse—his strategy had to be built on these.

He began looking for the surrey, hoping it had gone out of sight beyond the cottonwoods of the creek. But they had come quite close to it. Standing up, Holly was driving desperately along the creek bank, hunting a place where he could cross. Jim could see Hester looking back.

Well, if the gun could not do it, the horse would have to. He stretched himself along the pony's neck and let it have the bit. He could feel it surge ahead. Sorrell, riding hard as he tried to get past Jim, had a good lead, but the bay began to cut it down. Suddenly Jim saw that he and Sorrell were going to meet at the apex of the angle of their courses. Sorrell's horse was playing out. He quirted it with the stock of a rifle but its gait chopped, short and uneven. He was not going to take time for another shot, Jim saw, and he dropped Fowler's gun and drew his Colt.

Without warning Sorrell curbed his horse. It cut to a stop with its hind legs tucked under it. Sorrell snapped his rifle to his shoulder. He sat rock-still. Jim could see his face, the dark tape of his mustache and the smudge of beard on his jaws, the hard and steady eyes behind the sights. He raised the Colt, but thought, *He can't miss.* It seemed to him that he could see down the barrell of Sorrell's rifle. He fired hastily. His shot was high. The pony pitched and he had to seize the horn. Just then Sorrell fired. The bullet seared across Jim's back. It felt like a running iron laid red-hot on his coat. It scorched and cut and knocked the wind out of him.

Jim controlled the horse. He raised the gun again, wondering why his body did not react to the fact that he had been badly wounded. But his hand was steady, and he made this shot slow and sure, because he might never fire another. They said you did not aim a

Colt; you merely pointed it like your finger. But if the shot had to be as right as this one, you damn well better aim it. So he let the barrel settle and tried to ignore Sorrell's gun, cocked and ready. They both held this tiny coin of time and they had to spend it wisely. He could see a shine of sweat on the rancher's brow.

Jim felt the Colt kick at the heel of his hand. He saw Sorrell jolt back against the cantle. He saw his face change, loosen, and then with a great force of will set in stolid lines again. But the gun wavered. It crashed, and Jim thought he felt the impact of the muzzle-blast. The roar deafened him, but the bullet struck the ground beneath his horse. The horse pitched, and after he quieted it and could aim again he got Sorrell in his sights. The big man had dropped his carbine and was clinging to the saddle-horn with both hands. Jim saw his face begin to loosen again, blood dripped from his lips and stained the front of his shirt. Sorrell looked at Jim. He seemed bitterly to regret the proposition that he was beaten.

He started to wipe his mouth. But he lost his balance and fell to the ground. He got onto his hands and knees and clutched at the trailing reins of his pony. Then his right arm gave way and he lay with his cheek pressed against the earth.

Blood was running down Jim's back under his shirt. He gazed across the creek at the dust raised by the surrey. Holly had crossed. Jim could not bear the thought that Hester was going away from him. He wanted to ride after her, but he was too depleted. He sat on the ground near Tom Sorrell. After a time he raised his head and saw that the sun had fallen behind the mountains. An amber light tinted the air, as soft as lamplight. The wind had scoured everything clean. It was so quiet, so peaceful, that he wished it could go on forever.

At last he got up. He caught his pony but had to rest before he could mount. He jogged slowly toward the ranch, while dusk brushed the hills with lavender. He forded the cold, clear currents of the stream. Just before dark he heard a buggy coming. He reined up and waited. Then he called, and the buggy came on faster. Out of a grove of pinons, hazy in the twilight, a surrey came rattling, with Bill Holly driving and Hester beside him. Two other men, armed, rode beside the buggy. Holly peered up at Jim.

"You'd better climb off that horse, mister, before you fall off," he said. "Heard the shooting. What happened out here?"

"Tom Sorrell shot Anders. It wasn't much loss. Crowley thinks Anders may have killed Mr. Travis—we'll find out soon enough. And Sorrell wouldn't quit, so I did for him."

Holly grinned at him as he swayed in the saddle. "Whatever else you are, you're a stayin' dog, Harlan. Help him down, boys."

They helped Jim from the saddle. Hester watched silently. "Bill," she said, "couldn't you ride Jim's pony in? I'll drive Jim. Perhaps you'd all better round up the ponies and take care of Mr. Sorrell and Chet."

She turned the buggy and they drove along the stony, tilted road to the ranch. "Your lady friend," she told Jim, "is settled in her room. But I think you ought to decide how you want her shipped."

"However's quickest," Jim said. "Now that she's a widow, she'll want to go home to her folks as soon as possible. I feel sorry for her. But I don't reckon that's the same as love, is it?"

"I shouldn't think so."

"No," Jim agreed. "But I still need that right-of-way from you."

"Oh?" she said. "Are you still building a railroad?"

"Under new management." He explained it, and waited.

"That sounds quite sensible," she decided. "I certainly couldn't turn down old friends like Clancy and Day."

Jim settled forward on the seat. His back was tender and the rocking of the buggy tormented him. "I'm going to order a mahogany tie after we get started. It will be the first one we lay, and I'm going to do some pocket-knife carving on it: Two hearts and an arrow. Underneath that I'm going to carve, 'Jim loves Hester.' And every track walker for the next hundred years will say to his buddy, 'I wonder who Jim and Hester were?' "

"Who were they?" Hester smiled.

"Well, Jim was just a man with a pocket-knife and a hankering," Jim said. "But Hester was special—the kind of girl a man would buy a mahogany tie for, to tell her he loved her."

"That would be very nice," Hester said. "But would it be right to leave a hundred years' of track walkers in doubt? Certainly not. So a little farther on I want you to lay another tie of New Mexico juniper. And on that I'll carve, 'Hester loves Jim.' So then everyone will know. And I do want them to know, because it's so important. Now do you feel like kissing me?''

He did. He kissed her hungrily. Her lips were cold from the wind, but they soon warmed. And that was how they drove into the ranch yard, their lips touching, the tired horse plodding until it reached the corral, where it stopped, drew a deep sigh and let its head hang. Somewhere in the ranch house a clock softly chimed the hour. The notes sounded mellow and beautiful, part of the evening, part of their mood, and it was a long while before they left the buggy to go inside.